Buffalo Wolf

John Creed is a loner, a buffalo wolf – till he meets Polly Chantry. Each of them has a reason to be making their separate ways from Tamarack Creek to the diggings. Creed has letters to deliver, Polly is looking for her father. Then fate throws them together as they struggle to get through.

At the diggings they meet with Timber Wolf Flynn and his Sauk wife, White Fawn, but there is no sign of Polly's father. Creed and Polly set out on a double mission; to find Polly's father and acquire weapons to help the prospectors fight off the increasing threat from outlaws.

Their quest leads them high into the mountains and a frightening discovery at Gaunt's Peak. From there the trail leads to an unexpected encounter with the Sioux and another confrontation with the outlaws, before the decisive showdown and a shattering denouement back at the diggings. At the end, will Creed still be a buffalo wolf?

Buffalo Wolf

Colin Bainbridge

A Black Horse Western

ROBERT HALE

© Colin Bainbridge 2016
First published in Great Britain 2016

ISBN 978-0-7198-2103-5

The Crowood Press
The Stable Block
Crowood Lane
Ramsbury
Marlborough
Wiltshire SN8 2HR

www.bhwesterns.com

Robert Hale is an imprint
of The Crowood Press

Typeset by
Derek Doyle & Associates, Shaw Heath
Printed and bound in Great Britain by
CPI Group (UK) Ltd, Croydon, CR0 4YY

CHAPTER ONE

John Creed was at a loose end. The young lady who had attracted his attention the day before was absent from the breakfast room, so when he had drunk his last cup of coffee he wandered outside. It was just as well. He was passing through. Still, she hadn't been easy to ignore. Down the street he could see the old man dusting the boardwalk outside the stage depot; he meandered in that direction. When he got there the oldster looked up over his broom.

'I got me a problem.'

'Yeah? What's that?'

'The wagon's ready with the mail, but I ain't got nobody to drive it.'

It was early morning and the street was deserted. The old man spat into the dust.

'Unless you fancy taking it out, sonny?'

The person he addressed was in his early twenties.

Creed walked around the small wagon and examined the horses.

'Give me ten minutes,' he said.

He turned on his heel, walked back up the street and entered the Ground Hog Hotel. In five minutes he reappeared carrying a roll, a sheepskin jacket and a Paterson rifle. These items he slung into the wagon, alongside a number of sacks that were lying there. His six-guns were slung low, tied with rawhide thongs.

'How far and where to?' he asked.

'Just head for the diggings. Less than sixty miles.'

The old man went inside the building and returned with some blankets and a buffalo robe.

'Take these,' he said. 'I see you travel light and it can get real cold up in the mountains.'

Creed took them and threw them into the wagon alongside the other things.

'Appreciate it,' he said.

He stepped up on to the wagon box and flicked the reins. The horses strained and the wagon began to trundle slowly down the dusty street.

'Ain't you forgot somethin'?' the old man called.

'What's that?' Creed replied.

'Pay!' the man called. 'If you get back within the month it's one hundred dollars.'

Creed nodded.

'If you ever get back,' the oldster added beneath his breath. If the boy did return he calculated to be still well in profit at fifty cents for letters and twenty-five cents for newspapers, even allowing for the wagon and horses.

As the wagon rolled out of town Creed turned his head to take another look at its contents. The old man had included supplies. Creed had his own, anyway. In addition to the blankets and the buffalo robe, there was feed for the horses, and various other items were wedged in and lashed with ropes. With one hand he built himself a smoke. It was quite pleasant up on the wagon box with the early sun just gathering strength and a cool wind blowing from the east. Along about mid-afternoon he met two riders heading towards town, but otherwise the country seemed deserted.

It was flat here and featureless. He had no worries about getting the wagon with its team of four horses as far as the foothills, but the mountains were a different proposition. Even though he had taken the job on the spur of the moment, it never occurred to him not to see it through.

On the next day he saw the smoke signals. He did not have the knowledge to read them, but he figured they spelt trouble. But why would the Sioux bother about him? It would be sensible to be cautious. It was now mid-morning. The smoke signals continued, a single column followed by spherical clouds rising into the air. Then they ceased. Creed kept a watchful eye on the surrounding country. His rifle lay across his knee. It seemed to him that a strange intense silence lay across the prairie.

He stopped the wagon early in the afternoon and ate some pemmican washed down with water from the canteen. He took out his Colts, checked them and slid them back into their holsters. The chomp of the horses cropping the grass seemed unnaturally loud. The sun was hot and the landscape shimmered. A roadrunner crossed in front of the wagon and entered a thicket of thorny shrubs. The atmosphere was oddly hypnotic.

Soon he became aware of a distant drumming. At first it seemed to be inside his head but suddenly he realized that it was the sound of hoofbeats. Seizing the rifle he snapped to attention. Riding into view was a group of six Indian warriors. Their faces were painted and the leader, riding a white pony with a warpaint hand imprinted on its neck, wore a split-horn headdress and carried a lance lined with eagle feathers. He drew his sinewy horse to a halt, raised the lance, then lowered it again. Creed, placing the Paterson across his chest, held the upraised palm of his right hand towards the chief. The Sioux returned the greeting. *So far, so good*, thought Creed, *but now what?* The Indian turned and his glance swept the landscape in an inclusive gesture. Then, fixing the lance into the ground, he slid from his horse and approached the wagon.

Creed stood aside as the warrior began to riffle through the mail bags. The Indian drew a knife from a scabbard at his side, slit through one of the bags and emptied some of its contents on to the floor. He picked up first one of the letters and then another. Seemingly not able to make anything of them, he threw them back. He walked around the wagon, stopped to examine the horses, and stood face to face with Creed. For a few moments they regarded one another.

The Sioux chief had a broad forehead, high cheekbones and a strong nose. There was a resolute quality to his features. He nodded, turned and vaulted back on his horse. Taking up his lance, he muttered some words to the others, then turned again to Creed. With his forefinger pointing first to Creed, then to himself, he traced a rippling motion in the air. There could be little doubt that this signified the crawling movement of a snake.

Creed was thinking fast; a snake might mean an enemy, but the Indian had already returned his sign of friendship. His pointing movement was inclusive; maybe he was indicating a mutual enemy. Without further ceremony the Indians wheeled their horses and began to ride in the direction they had been following before coming upon the wagon. Creed watched them go. He was trying to puzzle it all out. The best he could come up with was that the Indians were giving him some kind of warning. Could they be trusted? He had liked the look of that chief.

The rest of the day passed without further sign of the Sioux. Creed was enjoying himself. So far this job was proving simple. He would deliver the letters and then pick up easy money at the end. He was in a state of limbo but the dice would have time to roll. For the moment he didn't have to think too much. Although it was autumn the days were mild. The landscape was still flat but varied with bushes and trees. Large balls of tumbleweed blew across the plains, sometimes spooking the horses.

Occasionally Creed came upon the vestiges of camps: objects that had been abandoned by migrants heading West. Some of these – mining tools, a book-case – he claimed for himself, thinking that they might come in useful. The bookcase he broke up for fuel to boil his battered coffee kettle. He was making pretty good progress and reckoned he would soon be among the foothills of the mountains.

On the next day he picked up sign of riders. He got down from the wagon and examined the ground carefully. It was well churned up. He calculated there must be at least a half a dozen horsemen. The horses were shod, so they were not Indian ponies. They had come down from the direction of the hills, in which case he was now ahead of them. He recalled the gestures of the Sioux chief. Could this have something to do with what the Indian had seemed to be warning him about?

Later that afternoon the wind grew stronger and big cumulus clouds began to fill the sky. Creed knew that he was in for a storm. Soon he could see squalls streaking towards him through the turbulent grey heavens. He jumped from the wagon and he did what he could to secure the contents, covering the bags of letters with the buffalo robe; then he took shelter underneath. The sky was almost black now, and the wind howled across the empty land. The rains swept in and Creed gathered his slicker around him. He was reasonably well protected but soon long streams of water were flowing beneath the wagon. The drumming of the rain was incessant and, high over the prairie, silver lightning forked across the sky. Thunder crashed and reverberated. Creed was concerned that the iron wheel-rims might attract the lightning and, reluctantly, he crawled out to take his place by the horses sheltering miserably behind some rocks. The storm was passing overhead. Again lightning flashed across the heavens, illuminating the landscape for a brief moment in an eerie blue glow.

For what seemed like hours the storm continued, but at length the wind and rain began to falter as the deep low tones of the thunder grew steadily fainter, rolling through the foothills. The storm was raging towards the south and east after beginning as snow in the mountains.

Just then the sun burst through a rift in the clouds

and across the heavily overcast sky a rainbow spread its radiant arch. From under the brim of his dripping hat Creed observed it with admiration. Then he rolled himself a cigarette.

The uplands here were crossed and scarred by run-offs and washes. After the rain the streambeds were babbling watercourses. The grass had become boggy and the horses' hoofs sank into the marsh. Creed was finding it hard going after the storm. Only when he had stopped to rest the horses did he become aware of an object in the distance. He took out his field glasses and trained them in that direction. It was a wagon and it seemed to be leaning over. Creed guessed that it had become bogged down in the soft ground. He looked again; the front wheels had sunk almost up to the axle. A figure appeared from around the side of the wagon and Creed involuntarily blinked.

'Goldurn it,' he muttered. 'It's a girl!'

Tugging on the reins, he turned his own wagon in her direction. He made slow progress and it was some time before she seemed to see him. When she did she disappeared into her wagon, then came back again carrying a rifle. She jumped down from the wagon box and, planting her feet firmly on the ground, she swung the gun towards him but pointed high.

'Hold it,' he called. 'I am a friend.'

The response was a shot, which went singing

harmlessly over the prairie.

'Now that ain't what I would call friendly,' he muttered.

He carried on in her direction, to be greeted by a second shot. Then he realized that she wasn't shooting in self-defence or in an effort to scare him off. On the contrary, she was signalling that she had seen him and needed help. In response he waved his hand and was rewarded by her waving back. She went back into the wagon, to reappear once more as he approached.

'Mister,' she said, 'I sure am glad to see you.'

Creed jumped down. To his surprise he recognized her. He had seen her only briefly at the Groundhog Hotel, but she was not the type to be easily forgotten.

'Stuck?' he said.

She nodded. 'Can't seem to make any headway. I was beginning to think I might not be able to make it any further.'

'Let's take a look,' Creed responded.

He climbed down and made his way to the back of the woman's wagon. The rear wheels were on firmer ground and she had already begun to unload the wagon in order to make it lighter.

'Give me a hand to unload the rest,' he said.

It took a while. There were trunks and boxes, some of them quite heavy, and several items of furniture. When they had finished he blocked the rear wheels, unhooked the traces and led one of the horses to the back of the wagon. He fastened a rope to each side of the axle underneath, then slapped the horse across the rump, tugging on the reins and encouraging it to pull. Fortunately the front wheels were not too firmly embedded; slowly at first but then with a jolt they came up out of the marsh. Then there came a loud snap and the wagon sank down.

'Hell!' said Creed. 'Looks like the whole wagon-box has collapsed.'

He glanced at the piles of equipment they had removed. 'Guess the weight was just too much.'

The girl looked at the discarded items, then back at him. Suddenly the edges of her mouth turned up and she laughed.

'I think you're right,' she said. 'So what do you suggest we do now?'

She said it in such an almost light-hearted way that Creed was taken aback, but he liked the way she seemed to include him in whatever action was to be taken. She certainly didn't seem to be fazed by the affair; which, to say the least, was unusual given that she was a lone woman stranded in a hostile country a long way from anywhere in particular.

Then he noticed the way her laughter had caused little dimples to appear on either side of her mouth. She was tall and had short black hair cut somewhat carelessly across her forehead and her eyes were a deep shade of blue. She wore a light-coloured riding habit and boots.

'There ain't any choice,' Creed replied. 'I guess you'll just have to ride alongside of me. We can hitch your horses together with mine, but I'm afraid you're gonna have to leave some of that merchandise behind.'

She hesitated for just a moment before replying.

'I believe you're right, in which case perhaps we'd better introduce ourselves. My name is Polyphema Chantry, Polly for short. And you're John Creed.'

He looked at her sharply.

'How did you know that?' he asked.

'Easy. I saw it in the hotel register.'

Why hadn't he thought of that? He wasn't sure how to proceed.

'If I'd have known you were headed this way too, I'd have come with you in the first place,' she said.

'It was kind of a snap decision,' he answered confusedly.

'They're always the best ones,' she replied.

He looked about. There were some low hills and, off to the right, a mesa indicated a possible river valley. He thought again of the indications he had found of riders. He was wary of being ambushed.

'Best be on our way,' he said.

After rerigging the horses he loaded the wagon as quickly as he could with Polly's assistance, transferring as many of her possessions as he thought the wagon could manage. There was a lot they had to leave behind.

'It doesn't matter,' she said. 'I was being too optimistic in the first place. Besides, most of it probably won't be needed.'

'I was wonderin' about that. The question seems too obvious to ask. What in tarnation are you doing out here?'

'I could ask you the same thing.'

'I'm headed for the diggings. There are letters in those bags I'm carryin'.'

'Then you're headed for the same place as me. And I bet my letter is in one of those bags.'

'Your letter?'

'The letter I wrote to my father telling him I was coming. But I suppose he'll already have it by now.'

'I wouldn't count on it. There hasn't been a delivery for a long time.'

'My father is a prospector. He reckons he'll make his fortune one day. He put me in a college back East but I've had enough of it, so I decided to come and join him.'

'What will he make of it? Your decision to come out West, I mean.'

'Oh, he'll probably not be very pleased, at least to start with. But I think I can soon win him round.'

Creed thought for a moment, looking at her.

'Yeah,' he said. 'I guess you probably can.'

*

16

The following day they were in the hills and had their first real glimpse of the mountains. From this distance the effect was magical. Like a battlemented wall of crystal they stretched across the skyline, the snow-capped higher peaks towering high into the air. It seemed that there could be no way through, but Creed knew there were canyons and passes that buckskinned mountain men had discovered and explored. Now the goldminers had arrived, Polly's father among them. Creed did not doubt but that he would find a route through to the diggings.

That evening they made camp by a brook flowing through hazel and dogwood thickets and overhung by a grove of aspen. It was cold now as a wind from the high country blew through the trees. Diamond points of stars filled the sky. Above them the slopes of the hills were clothed with dark stands of pine and spruce. Using some pine needles, Creed rubbed down the horses, then fed them with corn the oldster back in town had provided. He gathered some bark, leaves and dry branches and soon had a small fire blazing, with strips of bacon sizzling over the flames. He filled the kettle with icy water from the brook to make coffee. It tasted good.

Firelight flickered and danced among the shadows beneath the slender aspen trunks. Leaves rustled overhead. Somewhere nearby a hoot owl called its lament. From time to time the horses snickered or stamped and the wagon was a dark shape against the blackness of the trees. Creed gave the girl his sheep-skin coat and the buffalo robe. It was cold now, but it would be so much colder in the mountains and on the higher wind-swept peaks. He added some sticks to the fire and drank more coffee, folding his fingers around the tin cup. He picked up the Paterson rifle and checked that there was a round in the firing chamber. The girl observed him across the flames of the fire.

'Are you expecting trouble?' she asked.

'I'm always expectin' trouble.'

'I was scared,' she said. 'Not long after I had started from town I saw smoke.'

'That was the Sioux,' Creed replied. 'I came across them but they ain't the ones to worry about.'

'Then who is?'

'I don't know. I think the Sioux were trying to warn me about something and I saw tracks. I think whoever it is has been causing them trouble. If I understood their chief correctly, then we have a common foe.'

She reached for the pot and poured more coffee for them both.

'I'm glad you're here,' she said. 'I didn't have any idea of what to expect when I hired the wagon and set off from town. I think I must have judged things here by the standards that apply back East. I really don't know what I would have done if you hadn't have come by.'

Creed thought for a moment. He didn't want to scare the girl but he wanted her to have some inkling of how things stood. Instead of confiding to her his present concerns he opted for a more general statement.

'Things is different here in the West,' he said. 'It ain't the place for a lady to be settin' out on her own.'

'Yes, I think I realize that now.'

'Well, we'll push on into the high country tomorrow. With any luck you should be with your father soon.'

Shortly afterwards the girl retired for the night and was immediately asleep. Creed sat up for while. He was about to turn in himself when he heard the horses shifting their feet. He picked up his rifle and listened carefully. He could hear the drum of hoofbeats. They were some distance away but sound carried through the still night air. The pair of them were camped in a hollow and Creed felt fairly certain that the fire was screened.

After checking that Polly was still asleep he crept into the shelter of the trees to wait and watch. The hoofbeats grew louder, then began to diminish. Soon he could hear nothing further. Still he waited. Their own horses had settled down. Satisfied that whoever it was had ridden away, he emerged from the trees and resumed his place by the fire. He considered dousing it, but the night was too cold and he was confident it would not have been seen.

It was difficult to tell, but the sounds he had heard indicated a number of riders. They were probably the same ones whose sign he had detected. Otherwise it would seem too much of a coincidence. He wondered what they were doing. It was a strange time to be riding and he could not imagine that they were up to any good. Certainly for the rest of that night he would sleep light even if the cold were not so intense. He pulled his blanket over him, stretched out close to the fire and sought sleep.

When he awoke it was to find that Polly was already up and preparing breakfast.

'You shoulda let me do that,' he said.

She came towards him, carrying a tin mug of coffee.

'You must have been really tired,' she said. 'I thought I'd let you sleep on awhile.'

'I suppose I must have been. I don't usually lie long. It could get to be a dangerous habit.'

They sat together, enjoying the breakfast she had made and the cool crisp freshness of the morning. It was tempting to stay awhile but Creed was keen now to get to the diggings. When they eventually got under way, he looked out for traces of the riders he had heard during the night, but could see nothing. They must have travelled along another trail, but moving in the same direction up into the mountains. That meant they were still ahead of him.

The mountains, clothed with pine forests on their lower slopes, reared high above them. As Creed and Polly got closer they could see that the slopes were slashed with gulches and canyons. Waterfalls cascaded down their steep sides. The air held a tangy aromatic sharpness quite different from the air of the plains.

As they progressed the trail they were following became steep and rocky. Rugged outcroppings lay across their path and seemed to block the wagon's passage, but the way wound round them and then continued. The wagon splashed through small streams and rivulets coming down from the mountains and ahead of them the trail curved slightly before running downhill for a short distance and then rising steeply towards a shoulder of rock.

As Creed turned the wagon something thudded into the seat near his leg and a booming shot rang out, reverberating through the mountains. Without a second thought Creed seized his rifle and flung himself from the driver's seat. He reached up to help the girl to come down and they both took cover behind the wagon. Seconds later a further shot rang out and a bullet ricocheted from the iron rim of the front wheel, then went whining away into the woods. The girl gasped but she did not scream or show signs of panic. Creed was impressed. He gestured for her to stay low and looked about him.

He knew where the shots had come from. He

cocked the hammer of the Paterson and prepared to squeeze the trigger. He knew he had no chance of hitting anyone but the shot would act as a kind of warning. Then his finger relaxed. It might be better to leave them uncertain about whether they had hit him. It might be wise, too, to conserve ammunition. Where he lay he had good cover; he had the girl to worry about but he wanted to take the fight to them.

He decided to get into the trees. From there he could move up and outflank the attackers. Then he had another thought. If the bushwhackers were on the slopes above the outcrop, they had probably left their horses nearer the trail. If he could make his way through the pines undetected he could simply wait until they returned. The roles would be reversed. He was smiling now. They had missed their chance and he would make them regret it.

He waited patiently, but there were no further shots from the mountainside. Either they assumed they had killed him, or they were working their way around to another position. He and Polly were pretty well covered by the wagon, which filled most of the trail. In a few words he indicated to Polly what his plan was.

'Just don't move. I'll be back soon,' he said.

She seemed to catch on quickly and nodded in agreement. After checking his weapons Creed crawled out from the cover of the wheel and slithered quickly into the shelter of the pines. Once there he rose to his feet and moved swiftly up the slope. He was wary. He could not be sure if the marksmen had moved closer. When he judged he was sufficiently high, he began to circle towards the outcrop. Flurries of snow drifted down through the trees, but it was powdery and light.

Holding the rifle muzzle down, he paused behind the black trunk of a pine tree. He listened carefully for any sound but there was nothing that he could detect; just the cold wind stirring the leaves. He worked his way steadily forward and upwards until at length, through a gap in the trees, he could see a shoulder of rock below him. At first glance he could see no sign of horses, but as he crept forwards and gained a different angle he could see them knee-haltered in a space behind the rock and partly sheltered by an overhang.

As he had surmised, there were two of them. All his senses alert, Creed moved to a position behind a tree that gave him a clear view of the horses and settled down to wait. He had a fairly clear vision in all directions, so there was little chance of the gunmen surprising him.

The minutes passed. Still he could see or hear nothing that might indicate the gunmen's presence. He had learned patience, however, and the waiting did not bother him. He did not take unnecessary chances. He began to be conscious of the cold. Then a twig snapped and he fixed his hold on the gun action. Coming through a gap in the trees were the two gunmen. They were moving quickly and looking around them as they descended the slope. The horses snickered and shifted their feet. The men came close to the tree behind which Creed was concealed. As they passed he stepped out.

'Make one move and I'll blow your heads off,' he snapped.

They froze in their tracks.

'Throw your rifles aside and unbuckle your gun-belts.'

They made to do as Creed commanded, then suddenly it all changed. One of the men threw his rifle aside but the other man spun and fired. Creed felt the shock as the bullet thudded into the tree trunk, inches from his head, and fragments of bark flew up into his face. Almost at the same moment his own rifle spat lead and the man crumpled to the ground. The other, taking advantage of the sudden burst of activity, drew his pistol and fired, throwing himself aside, gun flaming.

That was probably his undoing because, as he had been unbalanced, the shot flew wide and before the man could recover Creed had slammed a couple of slugs into his hide. Gunsmoke filled the air and the horses down below began to blow.

Creed quickly took cover behind the tree and waited. He was pretty sure that both the gunmen were dead, but he wasn't going to expose himself till he was certain. The minutes dragged by and there was no movement. The snow had stopped now and only a dusting of it lined the trunks and branches of the trees. It was gloomy among the evergreens. Still he waited, until he was satisfied that his attackers no longer posed any threat, then he came slowly out from behind the tree.

Colt in hand, he approached the dark shapes slumped on the ground. He prodded the bodies with his toe, ready to shoot if necessary. He rolled them over. They were both dead, their eyes open wide as if surprised by what they no longer saw. Who were they? Why had they attempted to kill him? When he had stepped from behind the tree and challenged them he had hoped he might find the answers. Now he was faced with the question of what to do with them. He couldn't be too far now from the diggings. Maybe he should lift the bodies on to their horses and take them with him. Maybe he should try and bury them.

In the end he did neither. He had enough problems to deal with. Taking their weapons with him he walked down through the trees to the horses. At his approach they backed off, snorting, but he managed to quieten them and then lead them back along the trail to where the wagon stood. Polly was still crouched behind the wagon wheel but got to her feet as he approached.

'Are you all right?' she asked.

He nodded but at the same moment felt pain in his head and a sudden grogginess.

'You're bleeding!' she exclaimed.

For the first time he became aware of blood flowing down his cheek. He reached up and felt a long gash across his forehead.

'It's nothing,' he said. 'Must have got cut by some splinters of bark.'

'Let me take a look.'

'Sure, but let me see to these horses first.'

He dropped the reins and reached into the wagon for a bag of hay. He fed the horses and fastened them behind the wagon. He examined their own horses, which still stood in the traces, and satisfied himself that they had come to no harm. He fed them too. He placed the guns he had taken in the wagon and reloaded his own weapons. Then he returned to where Polly was waiting. He sat down while she bathed his face with water from the canteen and applied iodine from his medicine bag to the cut on his forehead.

'Who was it?' she asked.

'I guess some of the same varmints the Indians warned me about,' he replied.

'Why would they attack us?'

He shook his head. 'Maybe they didn't want us to reach the diggings,' he said.

He looked her over, not wishing to say that she might have been the one they were interested in. He was feeling better, although he realized that, quite apart from the cut, he was not entirely well. The rigours of the journey had caught up with him and he had maybe picked up some kind of a fever.

'Come on,' he said. 'There's folk waitin' to receive their mail.'

She gave him a long glance and smiled.

'You don't give a lot away, do you?' she said.

'What do you mean?'

'Oh, I don't know. Just a feeling I have.'

They climbed up on the wagon seat and Creed shook the reins. The wagon jerked forward.

'Keep your eyes open on that side,' Creed said.

She hadn't asked about his encounter with the bushwhackers. Her incuriosity appealed to him. He felt comfortable with her by his side. They rumbled on, alert for any further signs of danger.

As they rounded a bend in the trail they were surprised by a magnificent view. Creed drew the horses to a halt. On their left the mountainside fell away steeply to reveal a great panorama of high snow-capped mountains and deep canyons. Range upon range was revealed, magnificent and awesomely beautiful. Something inside of Creed had always wanted to be like those mountains: high, impregnable and alone. Now he wasn't so sure.

'It's wonderful,' Polly said.

'Sure is a mighty fine country.' For the first time Creed found himself glad to have someone with whom he could share it all.

Early the next day they had their first sight of the diggings. At this point the trail divided. One part continued uphill and the other branched off, leading downwards. Creed climbed from the wagon and walked a little way down the new trail to investigate. As he came round a corner he could see that it led to a narrow valley with a stream running through it. Part of the valley still lay in the shade of the mountain that towered above it. Near the river he could see the white shapes of bleached canvas tents and some scattered log cabins and shacks. Wisps of smoke curled from a few chimneys. There were piles of gravel and the small figures of people could be seen around gravel spits in the river. From this distance it looked an almost cosy scene. He looked round as footsteps signalled the approach of the girl.

'My father is down there,' she said. 'Maybe he's one of those people we can see by the stream.'

'We'll soon find out,' he replied.

The trail down was steep at this point and narrow, although it appeared to flatten out towards the bottom. Creed wasn't sure he could get the wagon down there, but since it seemed to be the main route into the valley, at least from this direction, he assumed it could be managed. The miners had got their materials in, after all. The two of them turned back and, before resuming his place on the box seat,

Creed attached chains to the wagon to help restrict its forward momentum. It was a little difficult to manoeuvre the wagon and the horses, but with his hand on the brake they started on the downward path.

It was a hard trail, but proved less problematical than Creed had feared, opening out and becoming less steep as they approached a grove of silver fir at the bottom. The valley was in a beautiful location, nestling among high peaks and snow-capped mountains and protected from the icy winds of the high ridges. They began to pass by some of the outlying tents and shacks, but most of the others were clustered together in a rough-and-ready camp near the river.

The track led in that direction and as Creed and Polly progressed some of the prospectors looked up to observe their passage. Most of them were too busy, some standing in the river and panning for gold, others shovelling dirt or operating narrow wooden troughs along which water from the river was diverted. Away from the river some men were probing at rocks with knives. There were narrower tributaries along which the same processes seemed to be going on.

It was a busy scene, contrasting strongly with the emptiness of the prairie and the loneliness of the mountain trail. Polly had become quite animated and was observing everything with keen eyes, anticipating that the next person she saw could be her father. Driving by tents that appeared to be empty, Creed continued past some further shacks and then drew the wagon to a halt outside a structure that was part tent and part cabin with a log frame. It had windows with no glass, and a canvas door. As Creed climbed down from the wagon box a man emerged and stepped towards him. He was large and heavily bearded.

'Looks like you hit some hard travellin',' he said.

'Guess you could say that.'

The man looked towards the wagon and the girl sitting on the box seat.

'Better come inside,' he continued.

As Creed moved forward he swayed. He would have fallen had the man not grabbed his arm. He put it round his own shoulders and helped Creed into the building, where he collapsed on a chair; Polly followed close behind. The man disappeared and then returned with a bottle of whiskey and a glass. He poured a generous measure.

'Get this down you,' he said.

Creed took it in one long swig and winced as the burning liquid went down his throat. He shook his head.

'Thanks,' he said.

It made him feel better, but not much. All the rigours of the journey had caught up with him. He felt exhausted and feverish.

'What you got there in the wagon?' the man enquired. 'Apart form the girl, that is.'

'Letters.'

'You come up from Tamarack Creek?' the man said in a wondering voice.

He took a long look at the youngster slumped in the chair and then another at the girl.

'Well, I reckon we can hear the details later. Right now I reckon you could both do with a little rest and recuperation.'

'I'm all right,' Polly said. 'I'll take care of him.'

'He's got a bad cut there,' the man said. 'We'd better get him into bed and find a doctor.'

Creed made to stand but fell back again.

'What about the letters?' he mumbled.

'Don't worry. The letters will be fine. Leave all that to me.'

After helping Creed to his feet the man assisted him across the room and through an open door into another room at the back. It was empty but for a bed with some stained and torn blankets.

'It ain't much, but you're welcome to it.'

He laid Creed carefully on the bed and covered him with the blankets. Creed lay back as he felt the room start to revolve around him. He was dimly aware that the man had left and that he was alone with Polly. He felt hot and cold at the same time and he was shivering.

'The letters,' he mumbled, 'must get the letters.'

31

He tried to sit up but fell back again. He felt Polly's cool hands on his head and then it seemed as if he was rolling down a long white slope before things went dark and he reached the bottom.

CHAPTER TWO

Creed awoke with light streaming through a window high in the wall and through the partly opened door. His head hurt and he felt weak. At first he did not know where he was but slowly his memory began to return. He tried to sit up but fell back again. He looked round the room and found that even moving his head required an effort. The room was bare of any furniture apart from the bed. On the wall facing him hung a faded tinted engraving representing Indians on horseback pursuing a buffalo.

Any further observations were interrupted as Creed heard heavy footsteps approaching. The door was flung wide by a figure whom Creed recognized as the man he had met on arriving at the mining camp. He could see now how big the man was. At least six and a half feet tall, he wore a shaggy red beard streaked with grey and his long hair curled over the collar of his check shirt. In his hand he carried a bowl of broth.

'Here,' he said. 'Get this down you.'

He sat on the side of the bed and made to assist Creed, but Creed brushed him aside with a wave of the hand.

'Just help me sit up,' he said. 'I think I can manage after that.'

Once he had been helped to a sitting position he tipped the bowl up and swallowed some of the broth.

'Hell!' he exclaimed, clutching at his throat and pulling a wry face. 'What in tarnation is that?'

The big man laughed.

'Indian broth,' he said, 'guaranteed to knock over a grizzly bear. Finish the rest of it.'

Creed did as he suggested. It tasted foul and burned its way like liquor down to his stomach, but he had to admit he already felt stronger.

'Wife's recipe,' the big man said. 'She's a Sauk'

'Well, I sure am grateful. Name's John Creed.' He held out a hand and the other took it and squeezed. Creed flinched.

'And I'm Flynn, Timber Wolf Flynn.'

Creed gave him a puzzled look.

'Can't hardly remember my real name,' the man said. 'It's been so long since anybody used it.'

Creed let it pass.

'Lookin' at you, I'd say you'd had a bit of an argument with someone,' Timber Wolf went on.

34

Creed nodded. 'A couple of bushwhackin' varmints. They came off a lot worse.'

'Well, we're mighty grateful to you for bringin' in the mail,' Timber Wolf said. 'I reckon as how you're going to be right popular round here.'

'I won't stick around for long,' Creed said. 'Just give me another few hours and I'll be OK.'

'You know how long you've been here?' Timber Wolf asked.

Creed looked at him.

'Two days,' the big man told him. 'You had a fever. For a lot of that time it was touch and go. If it weren't for that young lady of yours I don't know as how you'd have pulled through.'

Creed rested his head back against the wall and thought about what he had just been told. He didn't know what to say.

'Thanks,' he responded at last.

'Don't thank me. Like I say, the young lady is the one as sat with you and pulled you through.'

Creed reflected on these words for a few moments, until the man spoke again.

'She was askin' me about her father.'

Creed felt suddenly guilty, although he had been in no condition to concern himself about the matter.

'She came a long way to find him,' he said.

'Well, I guess that's just the point. He ain't here.'

Despite the pain in his head Creed jerked upright.

'Not here? She seemed pretty convinced about it.'

'He was here. Seemed a nice feller. He pulled out a couple of weeks ago.'

'Did he say where he was headed?'

'Not to me. I've asked around and it seems like he never told nobody else neither. Folks come and go. That's the way it is.'

'What was he ridin'?'

'He came in with a mule but he left it behind for someone. Seems he bought himself an old paint and just rode on out.'

Creed tried to focus his scattered thoughts.

'Polly must be upset,' he said. 'She set a lot of store on seein' her old man.'

Timber Wolf remained silent for some moments.

'Anyway, looks like you're over the worst,' he said at last. 'You just rest up now.'

He went back outside with the empty bowl and soon afterwards Creed slept again. When he woke up Polly was sitting on his bed, looking down at him.

'How are you feeling?' she asked.

He closed his eyes and then opened them again. His head had ceased pounding and when he attempted to sit up he experienced no discomfort.

'I'm fine,' he replied. He looked into her eyes. 'I gather I've got you to thank for looking after me.'

'No thanks needed. Besides, it wasn't just me tending to you. That Mr Flynn and his wife did their fair share. I believe you've met Mr Flynn?'

'Yeah. I've experienced his wife's soup too. Now

there's somethin' a lot of folk would like the recipe
to.'

She laughed gently. As if in response to their conversation there came a knock on the door. Timber
Wolf Flynn appeared with another bowl of the broth.
He set it down but left to tend to the store, saying
nothing. Polly made to ladle the soup into Creed's
mouth but he waved her aside.

'I think it's about time I started fending for myself
again,' he said. As he took the bowl he looked at her
and noticed the sadness in her eyes.

'Timber Wolf told me about your father,' he said.

She pulled her mouth into a firm line and was
quiet for a moment before responding.

'I can't believe it,' she said. 'To come all this way
and then just miss him. If only he'd got my letter
earlier.'

'I'm real sorry.' She was trying to put a brave face
on it but she could not prevent a tear escaping from
her eye. Creed was oddly moved.

'He can't have got far,' he said. 'Don't worry. We'll
find him.'

She looked up at him and there was such a look of
dawning hope on her face that he was glad he had
said the words.

'You must have your own plans,' she said. 'You
brought me here safely but I can't expect you to get
involved any further in my concerns.'

'I ain't got no plans,' he replied. 'There's nothin'

that can't wait.'

Suddenly she bent over and kissed him on the cheek; then, without further comment, she rushed from the room. Creed sat for quite a time staring at the picture on the wall. A mixture of emotions ran through him but at their core was a sense of pleasure and well-being such as he had not had before. He sat up and swung his legs over the side of the bed. Already he could feel a surge of strength returning to him.

Quickly, he made his way to where a water trough stood outside the store. Without pausing to examine the state of the water he climbed in and sank beneath the surface; it was icy cold but it felt good. When he had finished his ablutions he felt refreshed and animated. As he was drying off Timber Wolf came through the door.

'Looks like you're back on your feet again. Reckon you could manage an introduction to the place?'

Creed had assumed that Timber Wolf was a prospector, there for the gold, but it soon became apparent that the big man fulfilled a different role. The establishment was his and he ran the place as a combined store, hotel and trading post. The main room with the canvas door leading to the outside world was log-framed and, though sparsely furnished, was relatively luxurious compared with the basic conditions in which, from what Creed had observed while driving the wagon, most of the miners lived. The mantelpiece consisted of a beam of wood covered in tin strips made from cans hammered flat. The unglazed windows were covered in rose-patterned chintz. There was a threadbare carpet and some chairs, a table and a wooden bench. The floor was uneven so that the furniture tended to stand on three legs rather than four. Flowers – lilies, gentian, golden rod, blue penstemon and white violets – stood in pots and vases on whatever surface provided a space.

'Your wife?' Creed asked, indicating the display. Timber Wolf nodded.

'She's got a real taste for these things,' he said. 'Kinda nice, don't you think? She's probably out someplace right now, collecting more flowers. And herbs. You've got her medicine to thank for the way you're feeling now.'

They went through another open doorway into a room similar to the one in which Creed had been put; this one was piled high with food supplies. There were also various items such as metal bowls, wooden boxes, picks and shovels and other things that Creed couldn't quite place but which he guessed were to do with prospecting. From there they proceeded to the canvas part of the structure, which was bare apart from a trestle laid across a couple of barrels to form a rude counter.

'I've had my share of prospectin',' Timber Wolf said, 'and it's a fool's game. But I figured they all need to eat, they all need equipment. That's where the real pay dirt is.'

'What is the state of things round here?' Creed enquired.

'It's early days,' Timber Wolf replied. 'There's been some finds, but if it ever takes off they'll be up here in their thousands. Come on, let's take a look.'

Polly came from somewhere inside the building and joined them. She had resumed her normal attitude but Creed was acutely aware of her presence. They went outside. It was another clear, sharp day. Crystals of frost sparkled on the grass. Above the peaks hung some wisps of cirrus cloud.

'Good, isn't it?' Timber Wolf said. 'I don't reckon I could leave these mountains now. If the gold runs out I reckon I'll just go back to huntin' and trappin'.'

He paused, then went on: 'That's how I got me White Fawn. Cost me a lot of furs.'

Their way took them past empty shacks and tents. There was nobody around because they were all down either in the river or on the riverbanks.

'If there's any real gold it's likely to be way up in the mountains,' Timber Wolf commented. 'I figure the mother lode, if it exists, is somewhere back of Gaunt's Peak. That's the one you can see off to the north-west, the big one.' He indicated the mountain with his forefinger.

'Maybe there's a chasm up there containing ore, but it's going to be mighty hard ever to find it.'

He looked at Creed.

'Personally, I hope they never do.'

'Why?' Creed queried.

'Because if they do it will spell the end for this whole area, and I kind of like it as it is.'

'What do you mean?' Creed asked. He had a vision in his mind of the mountains as he and Polly had seen them coming over the trail.

'Look,' Timber Wolf said, pointing to where some miners were beginning to tunnel into a hillside some distance away. 'If they have their way, the mountain will be full of holes. Next they'll start hydraulickin'. I've seen whole hillsides removed and built up into dams. They'll need steam engines to pump out the shafts.

'Then they'll build more shafts, deeper shafts. Then the big companies will move in. The deep galleries will need to be supported. They'll need timber. Pretty soon whole forests will disappear. They'll build flumes down the slopes, they'll build pipes for water, they'll need access. That old trail you came in on ain't goin' to be much use to them. They'll blast out anything that gets in their way. Then they'll build crushing mills.' He turned to look again at Creed. 'See what I mean?' he said.

'Could result in a lot of business for you,' Creed replied.

'I got what I want,' Timber Wolf told him.

'Where would you go?'

'Somewhere. Maybe round here. There'll still be space.'

Creed stayed quiet. He did not imagine that Timber Wolf was normally a man much given to words, so he figured it made sense to listen right now.

By this time they were at the water's edge. As far as Creed could see, in either direction, men were working hard, dipping metal bowls into the sand and gravel of the riverbed. They would take the bowl out of the placer and swirl it around, gradually emptying out the sand and water. It looked like back-breaking work. Other miners, some of them in little groups, were making use of a rocker to try and extract any particles of gold, pouring water on to the dirt from the river in a sieve.

Timber Wolf led his visitors to another spot where a tributary stream came flowing in. Here a group of miners were gathered round a series of connected wooden troughs along which the waters of the stream were diverted by means of a wooden sluice. The waters ran into a contraption, the top part of which was an open-ended trough and the lower part a wooden box with cleats across the bottom. Some men were shovelling dirt into the trough, others were stirring it up. The finer sand was sieved through and any gold was caught against the cleats.

'Howdy!' Timber Wolf said. 'This here is John Creed and his girl Polly. John's the man who's brought us our letters.'

Creed glanced at Polly but she did not appear to be disconcerted. Some of the men looked up, others paused but soon resumed work. Creed observed that one of them limped badly.

'Appreciate it,' one man said.

'First mail in a long time,' another added. 'Nobody seems to want to make the run.'

'How'd they persuade you?' a third man asked.

'Didn't need no persuadin',' Creed replied. He peered into a riffle box.

'Any luck?'

'Nope,' the first man said. 'Down to our last pot of beans at this rate.'

As they walked away Creed asked Timber Wolf whether any of the miners had struck it rich.

'There's a fair amount of gold around the place,' Timber Wolf replied. 'A few prospectors had lucky strikes to set the whole shebang going.'

Creed looked away at the dazzling, distant Gaunt's Peak. It looked unreal, almost as insubstantial as the clouds that gathered about its slopes – and as likely to float away.

'The real gold is up there?' he said.

'That's what some folks reckon, but they could be wrong,' Timber Wolf told him.

They walked back past men waist-deep in the water.

'Seems to me there's plenty of scope for argument,' Creed said. 'How does anyone know where one claim starts and another ends?'

'They organize themselves. So far it seems to work. They've fixed the size of a claim. There's a list of them: matter of fact, I'm the recorder. It's only a few sheets of paper. They have regular meetin's. There's one tonight if you care to come along.'

'No thanks. Appreciate the offer but I don't plan to stick around too long now.'

'Might be of some concern to you.'

Creed paused to take a good look all around the camp.

'Don't reckon I'm cut out for prospectin',' he said.

'No, maybe not,' Timber Wolf replied. 'But I reckon you might be interested in findin' out more about a bunch of bushwhackin' skunks that nearly had your hide.'

'Bushwhackers?' Creed said.

'You mentioned somethin' about it when you first rode in. There wasn't much time for details.'

'What do you know about them?' Creed asked.

'I could be wrong, but it seems more than likely that they're connected with a gang of owlhoots who've chosen to nest up somewhere in the mountains. We've had some trouble. There's been shootin'. You noticed that man back there had a damaged leg? That was a gunshot wound. He shouldn't be up on his feet really, never mind workin' a claim. I reckon they're just bidin' their time.'

Creed was thinking fast. A gang of owlhoots? Could they have been what the Indian had been warning him against?

'I don't see why they would choose to pick on me,'

he said.

'It would fit the pattern,' Timber Wolf replied. 'So far we've had the odd shootin', mainly isolated incidents. Nobody's been killed up to now but things is goin' to get a lot worse.'

'Any idea who they are? Or how many there might be?'

'Outlaws, drifters, out-of-work range hands – anyone looking for a fast grubstake. It's just a guess, but I reckon there's probably already more than a couple dozen of 'em. And they're growin' fast. The mountains are a good hideout and now they can think about just pickin' off the prospectors.'

As they approached Timber Wolf's emporium the slender figure of a woman dressed in a blue gingham dress appeared at the doorway.

'Come and meet White Fawn,' Timber Wolf said. 'Folks around here call her Anna.'

Creed was struck with how petite she was. Alongside Timber Wolf she looked almost childlike. Timber Wolf made the introductions.

'Pleased to know you,' Creed said, and held out his hand. She responded by awkwardly holding out her own hand and their palms briefly touched. She looked up at Timber Wolf and said something in a language Creed did not understand.

'She can speak English, but she feels happier using her own tongue,' Timber Wolf commented. He listened to her closely, then turned to Creed.

'She says she is pleased to see you've made a good recovery.'

'Give her my thanks and tell her I really appreciate everything she's done for me,' Creed replied.

Timber Wolf laughed. 'Like I said, she understands English. Why not tell her yourself?'

Creed repeated what he had said, then smiled when he realized she must have understood it in the first place. White Fawn smiled in return and with an almost imperceptible movement of the head she said something to Timber Wolf. Then she skipped away with a graceful motion.

'She says there's coffee on the stove and flapjacks.'

'Sounds good to me,' Creed replied. He watched White Fawn as she walked in the direction of the river. She turned quickly once to look back at him.

The evening meeting took place out of doors. It was a perfect setting. Overhead the huge disc of the Milky Way seemed to float in the heavens and in the valley camp fires glowed. The mountains stood like sentinels, black against the sky. Frogs croaked near by and a whippoorwill called. From somewhere a fiddle's thin notes played a lonesome tune.

Creed was introduced and welcomed. He was a popular figure, having succeeded in bringing in the mail. It was the first contact many of the men had had with the outside world for a long time. It brought news from home, a reminder that another world still existed that did not consist of constant hard work and meagre rations. Timber Wolf had thrown a newspaper in Creed's direction. The headlines ran:

Republican Nominations
For President Abraham Lincoln of Illinois
For Vice-President Hannibal Hamlin of Maine

Neither name meant anything to Creed.

Before the main part of the meeting began several matters were resolved. There was a dispute about the rights to a claim. Each party stated its case and presented evidence. A witness was called for one side, and then another witness for the other side. In the end a vote was called. The losing party did not seem particularly put out at the verdict.

One man wanted to sell his claim and there ensued a dispute over the price. A miner named Josiah Bent explained to the company what had happened to him at a more remote stream bed. He had been working a placer when he had been set upon by some rowdies. It seemed to Creed that such minor problems probably arose from boredom. The men were without women and had little to do when not working but drink and gamble.

Timber Wolf seemed to be the only one with female company. Maybe it was just as well that White Fawn was shy, Creed reflected, though he imagined the big man would have little difficulty in taking care of things should they ever threaten to get out of hand.

During the course of the meeting the prospectors appointed a committee of volunteer vigilantes to keep order about the camp. That took them to the principal matter of what to do about the threat from the outlaw gang in the mountains but Creed left when they reached that point. He wandered away along the river till he found a quiet spot. The murmur of the men talking in the distance reached his ears and mingled with the soughing of the wind and the ripple of the waters. A few lights gleamed on the hillsides. He had begun to think about the events of the past few days when he heard a footstep. Looking up, he saw Polly approaching, carrying what looked like a piece of paper.

'Mind if I join you?' she said.

'Of course not. It'd be a real pleasure to have your company. What's that you got in your hand?'

'It's the letter I wrote to my father.'

'Mind if I take a look?'

She held it out to him and in the dim light of the stars he read the words:

Friday July 17.
I have had my last lesson with Miss Cripps and have already given notice to leave, so it's no use you trying to persuade me to stay. By the time you read this I will probably be on my way because I don't intend wasting

48

any more time. You see, Father, I am determined to come and see you. I have had enough of living back East. I can't say exactly when I will arrive at Tamarack Creek or how I will get from there to the diggings, but do not worry about me. I can take care of myself.

Your loving Daughter Polly.

'It sure is a shame that you just missed him,' Creed said.

'That's what I wanted to talk to you about. I had already taken the decision to try and find him before you made your offer. I really appreciate your concern, but after thinking about it I really can't expect you to throw everything up to start off on what must appear to be a wild-goose chase with someone you barely know.'

'Don't worry your head about that. I meant what I said. Now I've finished my business here we might as well get started just as soon as we can.'

She began to remonstrate but he cut her short.

'There's no point in talkin' about it any further,' he said. 'Besides, I kinda got a stake in all this. Timber Wolf said he thought your father was a good man. All these folk are out here to try and make somethin' of themselves. I've got to like them too, even though we've only been here a few days.'

She was silent, thinking hard.

'I don't know where to begin,' she said at length. 'I have no idea where he might have gone.'

Creed looked up towards the soaring summit of Gaunt's Peak.

'Timber Wolf said somethin' about the main lode maybe bein' up in those peaks,' he said. 'Maybe that's where we ought to start.'

'You think he might have gone up there?'

'If he wasn't havin' any luck down here and if he was of the same opinion, seems as good a place as any. If he's not there we'll try somewhere else.'

'He might have gone back to Tamarack Creek.'

'He might have, but you'd probably have picked somethin' up. It's a pretty small place.'

'Wouldn't it be ironical if we passed each other en route?'

Creed got to his feet. 'Let's just take it one step at a time' he said.

It was late now and the meeting seemed to have broken up. A few diehards still remained panning for gold in the darkness. Some campfires burned brightly, but most had died down to embers. The sky was filled to overflowing with a vast multitude of stars. As they walked towards the main body of the camp Polly looked upwards.

'The Sioux believe they are sky dust thrown up by spirit buffalo as they move across the heavens,' Creed commented.

'That's lovely,' Polly replied. She looked at him

50

and smiled. As they walked in a rambling sort of fashion a vague figure came towards him from further along the river. As it drew closer they recognized White Fawn.

'Hello,' Creed said as she approached. He wasn't sure just how much English she knew.

'It's a fine evening but you must be cold,' Polly said.

White Fawn was wearing the same gingham dress as earlier but had thrown a beaded robe over her shoulders.

'I think you both go soon?' she said.

'Yes,' Creed replied.

'Then you know what's going to happen.'

'Happen? About what?'

'Bad men cause trouble. At the meeting tonight it was decided we must fight them.'

Creed nodded. 'No-one wants trouble,' he said, 'but if trouble comes that is the best way to meet it.'

'Always trouble,' she said. 'Where I come from, trouble. Here, trouble.'

'You have a good man. Stay with him.'

'Yes, of course,' she replied. 'I think you good man too.' She hesitated before speaking again. 'When you go on journey?' she asked.

'Tomorrow,' Creed replied.

As she made to leave, Polly touched her shoulder.

'What do you like to be called?' she asked inconsequentially.

'My name here Anna. But my real name Anamosa. It mean White Fawn.'

'It's a nice name. And it suits you. I shall call you Anamosa.'

The Indian looked into Polly's face and smiled briefly. Then she was gone, moving lightly on her moccasined feet.

'She seems worried,' Polly said.

'I guess the prospectors can look after themselves,' Creed replied, although he wasn't too sure.

The next day came in with a flurry of snow. Timber Wolf stood looking up the trail.

'Weather's breaking,' he said. 'You might have problems getting through.' Creed had explained their plans and Timber Wolf had given them horses and provisions from his store. 'I think I should come. I know some of the trails.'

'You've plenty to do here,' Creed replied. 'Besides, you'd only slow us down.' They both laughed. 'Just look after things this end. Take care of White Fawn. She's all the gold you need.'

'I know it,' Timber Wolf replied.

Creed swung himself into the saddle and he and Polly began to move down the trail.

'By the way,' Creed turned to look back, holding his horse steady for a moment, 'I've been meanin' to ask you. . . .'

'What's that?' the big man replied.

'How do you get the name Timber Wolf?'

There was a moment's pause, then Timber Wolf burst into a roar of laughter. Some of the prospectors who had gathered to see Creed off joined in the amusement.

'It would take longer than we got,' the big man replied. 'I'll tell you some day – if you ever get back.'

'It's a deal,' Creed said. He turned again, pressing gently on the flanks of his mount.

He and Polly rode on, passing the lines of tents and shacks, the horses straining as the trail began to rise towards the mountain pass they had come down a short time before. As they rode higher they looked down on the camp. Creed could see the attractions that such a place would have for outlaws on the run, looking for easy pickings. He would be on the alert for any signs of them.

He wondered if there were other means of access to the valley. He guessed there were but had not thought to ask. In any event this route was the appropriate one. It was good to be astride a horse again, even though mules might have been more appropriate to the terrain.

Then he got to thinking about the valley, about the prospectors with their urge to seek gold, and about Timber Wolf. Timber Wolf was of a different generation but Creed sensed that he and the big man were from the same mould. Timber Wolf had become involved in running the store, but the spirit of the mountain man still burned in him. He found himself thinking about White Fawn and wondered whether they would see either Timber Wolf or White Fawn again.

CHAPTER THREE

The snow that had threatened to fall had not come but the skies were heavy. It was the wrong time of year to be riding the high country but there was nothing to be done about it. Creed's main concern was how Polly would cope, but then he reflected on how well she had done so far. They were sufficiently supplied and provisioned. If things got bad they could head back for the camp. There was no problem in finding directions: the great summit of Gaunt's Peak rearing its white cap into the sky was a clear landmark. Creed figured it would take no more than a couple of days' riding, maybe less if the weather held.

They made good progress and did not stop till mid-afternoon, when they made a brief camp before pressing on till nightfall. Creed found a sheltered spot and built a fire. Soon they had made themselves comfortable and were making the most of some beef hash that Timber Wolf had provided. Afterwards they sat by the fire and reflected on the progress they had made.

'Same again tomorrow,' Creed said, 'and we should just about be there.' The dark, towering shape of Gaunt's Peak reared over them.

'I like it in the mountains,' Polly said. 'I can see why my father would come here.'

'Guess he was hopin' to make a strike,' Creed said.

'Yes. It must have cost him quite a bit to keep me in that boarding school. I never really thought about it till now.'

Creed hesitated for a moment, then asked; 'What about your mother?'

'I never really knew her. She died when I was three. Seems like it was always just me and Father.' Polly looked across the fire at him. 'What about you? You're not much older than me.'

'I got folks but ain't seen 'em in a long time. Me and Pa had our differences. I lit out when I was sixteen and ain't been back or heard nothin' since.'

'Lit out from where?'

'Ozarks. Guess I'm a natural mountain man.'

The next morning, before they set off, Creed carefully removed any traces of the fire, keeping in mind the possible presence of the outlaws. As they progressed he was looking about for any sign that Polly's father had ridden that way. Suddenly he noticed something.

'Stop!' he said.

He dropped from the saddle and walked over to examine what he had seen. Polly dismounted and joined him.

'Horse droppings,' he said. 'Maybe three, four days old.'

Polly knelt down, excited. 'Do you think they could be from my father's horse?' she gasped.

Creed nodded. 'There's a chance,' he replied.

'A good chance? Who else could it be up here?'

Creed didn't want to worry her or say anything to dampen her enthusiasm, but at the same time she needed to be aware the dangers of their situation.

'Could be outlaws,' he said, 'but at least it looks like we might be on the right track.'

They remounted and moved on. The trail was leading them away from the giant Gaunt's Peak but they continued to follow it till eventually Creed's sharp eyes detected a narrow track leading off in the direction they wanted to go. Previous snow had blown across it and there were some deep drifts on either side.

'Take care,' he warned. 'Keep your horse away from the edges.'

Timber Wolf had chosen their mounts well; the horses were used to the mountains and they picked their way carefully across the treacherous terrain.

The riders moved on, only stopping to eat, as they had done the day before, until the rays of the setting sun began to touch the tops of the mountains in a roseate glow.

'Do you think we should stop soon?' Polly asked. Creed looked up towards Gaunt's Peak.

'Keep goin',' he said. 'We must be almost there.'

He wasn't sure what to expect but he figured that Polly's father probably wasn't the only one to have headed for the mountain. The fact that Timber Wolf had mentioned it at all as a possible site for the mother lode suggested that others had made it this far. He was right. Towards evening they topped the crest of a long rise and there below them were the scattered tents of a small settlement. Polly turned to Creed with a glow on her face and a sparkle in her eyes.

'I didn't expect there to be a camp,' she said excitedly. 'My father must be down there.'

Creed sat silent. As they had come higher up the trail he had observed sign of a number of horses having ridden in from a side trail. Looking down at the camp, he couldn't see any indication of movement or activity. Granted, it was on a much smaller scale than the other settlement but he would, even so, have expected to see the lantern lights of prospectors still at work in the gloaming. He reached for his field glasses and put them to his eyes. Polly, catching something of his disquiet, looked at him anxiously.

'What is it?' she asked. 'Shouldn't we be getting

down there?'

He grunted and held up his hand. Sweeping the camp with his glasses, he could see that some of the tents were torn and flapping in the breeze. The snow and mud were trampled in places, and there were hoofprints in the snow leading towards a flank of the mountain. The place appeared to be deserted except for a number of horses, which were standing in a crudely constructed corral.

'Something's wrong,' he said. 'I can't see anybody.'

'Maybe they've stopped for the evening.'

'There'd still be somebody about. Some of the tents have been damaged.'

'What do you think has happened?'

'I don't know.' He put the glasses back in their case.

'Only one way to find out,' he said. 'But be careful and do as I say.'

She gave him a startled glance.

'If anything happens, do as I say,' he repeated.

They rode down the long slope towards the camp, Creed's eyes and ears alert for signs of danger. Long shadows were spreading across the hollow and the vast bulk of Gaunt's Peak stood like a colossus astride their path. The horses were wary and tossed their heads nervously.

Polly rode her horse close up to Creed's. They were coming alongside the first of the tents. The flapping of the canvas in the wind was eerie and when they passed tents that had been ripped they seemed to speak of something untoward in sinister tones.

Creed stopped his horse and slid from leather. He peered inside a couple of tents. They seemed not to have been disturbed. Everyday items lay apparently unmoved and in one tent there was a meal standing untouched on a wooden box that served as a table. Creed mounted again and the pair of them rode through the little settlement till they reached the further edge.

Between the last tent and the forbidding wall of rock that formed the base of Gaunt's Peak there stretched a piece of open ground extending for about eighty feet. The snow there was churned and muddy and, when he looked more closely, Creed could discern the faded and snowed-over sign of bootprints. There were also a few remnants of hoofmarks, but Creed reckoned not more than two or three sets.

'Let's take another look,' he said. 'On foot.'

They climbed down and Creed hobbled the horses. When he had done so the two of them started to walk back the way they had come, stopping to look into some of the empty tents. It was the same story. Nothing seemed to have been disturbed but there was nobody about. It didn't take them long to reach the end of the row of tents and then retrace their steps. By the time they had got back to the horses the last rays of sunlight had disappeared from the mountain tops and the whole place was plunged in deep shadow.

'I don't like this,' Polly said. 'I think we should get out of here.'

'What about your father?'

'We've been up and down and looked everywhere. There's nobody here. The place must have been abandoned. Maybe they just realized that there was no gold to be found and moved out.'

'Without taking any of their things with them? Leaving their tents and all their equipment behind? I don't think so. And what about the horses? Some of them may be gone but there are others in the corral.' Creed was thinking aloud. Having spoken the words it became obvious to him who must be behind the state of things as they had found them.

'Those outlaw varmints!' he snapped.

'Outlaws?'

'Of course. The same ones as tried to bushwhack us. The same ones the Sioux warned me about. The same ones Timber Wolf and the rest of them are gettin' ready to fight.'

'We didn't see anything of them on the way up here.'

'Nope. That's because there are probably other routes into these mountains. Come on; let's go take a look around.'

He took his rifle out of its scabbard and moved away from the tented area, in the direction of the mountain. Polly clung to his arm. He got down on to his knees to examine the ground more closely.

'Looks like a group of men walked this way,' he said. 'As far as I can tell, they were movin' towards the cliff.' The sign was not good but it seemed to lead straight to the sheer face of Gaunt's Peak. 'I wish it was daylight. It's hard to see anything clearly.'

They were following the wall of rock. Here and there, so far as they could make out, an assault had been made on it with what Creed guessed were picks and shovels. The track was bending slightly to the right and as they came round a corner they could see piles of rocks that appeared to have fallen from on high. It wasn't until they reached the pile of boulders that Creed realized the rocks hadn't fallen but had been blasted from the cliff.

'Dynamite,' he said. They moved past the rocks to see a deep indentation in the cliff face.

'Looks like it could be the entrance to a tunnel.'

They looked at one another, the same thought occurring to them both.

'Maybe the prospectors got caught inside by a rock fall,' Polly gasped.

'Yeah, but I don't think it was accidental. They wouldn't all have been inside. Seems to me like they were brought here, put inside, and then the tunnel was dynamited.'

'But that would be cold-blooded murder.'

Creed shrugged. 'Isn't that what they tried to do to us?'

Creed moved inside what appeared to be the tunnel entrance. The roof was low and the space was blocked by rocks and debris. He began to tug at some of the stones but they were too big and heavy to shift.

'What are you doing?' Polly asked.

'They could be in there,' he said.

'You mean they might have been deliberately buried alive?'

'If the blast didn't kill them. And I don't know whether there'd be any air inside. But it's a chance.'

It took a moment or two for his words to sink in, but once she had assimilated what he was saying she seemed to gather herself together.

'Why don't we shout? If there's anybody in there they might hear us.' Without waiting for a reply she suited action to the words and began to call out loudly. When she stopped they listened, but could hear nothing. She repeated the exercise, shouting even more loudly, and Creed added his own voice. Then they ceased and listened once more.

When they still could hear nothing Creed drew his six-gun from its holster and fired into the air. He was hesitant about the noise they were causing but he was reasonably satisfied that there was no one about. If the owlhoots were indeed responsible, they seemed to have left the scene – probably some time before. The boom of the gun reverberated from the mountainside; they listened till the last echoes had died away.

'Listen!' Creed hissed. From somewhere in the depths of the mountain he thought he could detect a faint call. 'Can you hear it?'

'Yes. I think there is someone in there.' Polly's brow was lined in concentration. Creed started to pull at the rocks again.

'The question is,' he said, 'if there's anyone inside, how do we get them out?'

Polly joined him at his task, digging frantically at the pile of rocks and boulders. She succeeded in levering out some smaller pieces and Creed heaved hard to eject a few of the bigger ones, but it soon became apparent that the task was hopeless.

'We'll never do it this way,' Creed said.

'We must. We can't just walk away and do nothing.'

Suddenly Creed dashed his fist into the open palm of his other hand.

'Dynamite!' he repeated.

'What do you mean? We haven't got any dynamite.'

'No, but the prospectors had some. How else could they have created this tunnel? Quick, let's go back and take another look in some of those tents.'

Despite the darkness it took no time for them to make their way back to the camp and begin looking for sticks of dynamite. Time passed but they could find no trace of any.

'Wouldn't the prospectors have stored it somewhere else?' Polly asked. 'Surely it would be too dangerous to have it right on hand next to their living quarters?'

'Yes, you're probably right.' Creed stopped his search of the tent in which they were crouched. 'But where would it be?'

They both thought for a moment.

'I reckon they'd store it somewhere pretty close to where it was likely to be used,' Creed said at last. 'I think we should go back and take another look nearer the tunnel.'

They left the tent they had been searching. The clouds had parted to reveal stars and a scudding moon. Moving quickly across the intervening ground, they reached the blocked-up tunnel entrance again. Not having found anything new, they moved further round a projecting corner of the mountain rock.

'I think I see something,' Creed said. A dim shape was outlined against the lesser darkness surrounding it. 'It's another tent, but it's hard to make out because it's made of a darker material.'

Coming closer, they could see that the tent was marked with a large red cross.

'This must be it,' Creed said. Bending low, he undid the tent flap then went inside, followed by Polly. Stacked in one corner were the sticks of dynamite they had been looking for.

'Be careful,' Polly said. 'Are you sure you know what to do?'

'Yeah. I've used the stuff before.'

Having taken what he needed, Creed moved outside again. As he and Polly approached the jutting rock wall he turned to her.

'You'd better stay here,' he said. 'Take cover behind this outcrop. I'll go on and set the thing up.'

'Please be careful,' she repeated.

'Don't worry. I know what I'm doin'.'

He moved around the corner and quickly got back to the tunnel entrance. He wasn't as confident as he had made out. He had told Polly a white lie. He had been around people who had used dynamite but what he knew was based more on observation than experience.

After cutting the sticks in half he slid a cap into each portion before placing them all where he figured they would have most effect. Then he lit the fuses and ran for cover. The blue flames ran like snakes through the mud and snow, throwing out a trail of sparks, then there came an almighty explosion; rocks and boulders were flung high into the air and fragments of stone rained down near his head where he crouched beneath an overhang. His ears rang with the deafening noise and the air seemed to have been sucked from his lungs.

When the dust had begun to settle he emerged from his place of safety and ran towards where he had left Polly. He was relieved when he saw her emerge from behind the outcrop, holding her hands over her ears. They ran to each other and Creed held her in his arms. She was shaken and scared.

'It's OK,' he said. 'I think I maybe used too much.'

After a few moments they were sufficiently recovered to make their way to the tunnel. Where the blockage had presented what seemed an impenetrable barrier there was now a yawning gap. Part of the cave roof had fallen in and created a new blockage but there was plenty of space for them to walk through. Thick dust and smoke filled the passage and it was difficult to make anything out.

'Hell,' Creed said. 'I hope that whoever's in there was standing well back.'

They advanced a little way down the passage till it grew so dark that they couldn't see. Creed struck a match. They were in a very narrow tunnel, the roof of which was just above their heads. A little further on it dropped even lower. There were pools of water on the floor and water running down the walls. The match went out and again they were in darkness. They did not move, then Polly thought she heard something.

'Let's shout again,' she said.

They began to call, their voices sounding at once both loud and muffled. Presently they heard a faint answering call. It was hard to tell from which direction it was coming but after a few seconds other voices were raised in support. Then they could distinguish the sound of footsteps from further down the tunnel. Creed struck another match in time to see the first stooped figure emerge from the darkness.

'Who is it?' the man gasped.

'Friends,' Creed said.

He struck a further match. Several men had emerged from the tunnel, looking grimy and exhausted.

'How long you been in here?' Creed asked.

'Don't know. Must be days. We started lookin' for a way out. I don't think we coulda lasted much longer.'

Polly was looking at the worn and blackened faces of the men but as yet there was no sign of her father.

'Make your way back to the camp,' Creed said.

'Is there anyone left in there?' Polly added.

'There's a couple of wounded bein' helped along.'

'You blasted your way through?' the first man said.

'Yeah. Hope I didn't cause too much of a shock.'

In the light of the match the man grinned.

'Sweetest sound I ever heard,' he said. He held out a hand. 'The name's Blackstock. Whoever you are, I'm mighty glad to see you.'

After a short time the wounded men appeared, being assisted by a few of their comrades. When there was no one left Creed and Polly, accompanied by Blackstock who had remained behind to make sure the rest were accounted for, made their way out of the tunnel and back to the camp.

'Dolgurned rancid polecats,' Blackstock murmured. 'They deliberately rounded us up, put us in the tunnel and then buried us alive. I aim to get even for that.'

'You'll get your chance,' Creed replied.

'Do you know a man called Dan Chantry?' Polly asked. 'Was he in there with you?'

The man thought for a moment.

'Dan Chantry? Nope, don't know anyone of that name. Why? Who is he?'

'He's my father,' Polly said. 'We came here to find him.'

'You come up from the diggings?'

'Yes.'

'How's old Timber Wolf?' the man asked.

'He's fine.'

'Reckon I'm finished with this place,' Blackstock said. 'Mother lode or no mother lode, I'm headed back for civilization.'

'Don't forget you got a score to settle first,' Creed told him.

When they got back to the camp Creed and Polly, together with those who were least debilitated, made a fire and prepared a meal. The men had gone without food for several days. Fortunately the outlaws had not destroyed the camp and supplies had been left untouched. During the course of the meal the rest of the story was revealed. The prospectors had been taken unawares when the outlaws rode in. They had been rounded up, put in the mine, and the entrance dynamited. They had tried to find another way out but without the intervention of Creed and Polly they would have died a slow and agonizing death.

'I don't get it,' one of the men said. 'They didn't take nothin'. They left the place pretty much as they found it. What was the point?'

'Seems like they been gatherin' up in these mountains for some time,' Creed told him. 'They got to have a hideout somewhere. Maybe they figured you were gettin' too close to it.'

'That don't account for the way they treated us,' Blackstock said.

'They don't care. For them it was just a way of disposin' of an inconvenience.'

'I figure they did things the way they did so that if anybody came up here, they'd figure it was an accident.' Creed suggested. 'That would account for the horses bein' left.'

'Those animals could be in a bad way,' somebody opined.

'I'll see to 'em,' Creed responded. 'They probably found enough grass to get by on and there's no problem with water. Snow's standin' deep in parts.'

'So what do we do now?' another voice broke in. 'They might come back.'

'I doubt it,' Creed said. 'They think they've safely disposed of you. There's no call for them to return, leastways not for a time.'

'It's still too dangerous,' said Blackstock. 'There's not enough of us. I aim to get revenge on those varmints, but it's goin' to take more men than we got here.'

'I figure Timber Wolf and most of the others have a similar idea in mind,' Creed told him. He drew out his pouch of tobacco, rolled himself a cigarette and then handed the pouch to the others. 'I think the best thing would be for you all to return to the main camp,' he said. 'When you're back at the diggings, you could hold a meeting and decide what you do about all this.'

There was some discussion about the details, but in general Creed's suggestion was accepted as the only reasonable thing to be done.

'What about you?' asked Blackstock.

Creed turned to Polly, who was sitting by his side. She had been quiet and inattentive during the course of the conversation and he knew what was on her mind.

'We came her lookin' for Miss Chantry's father,' he replied. 'We figured he was up here with the rest of you. Apparently we were wrong. So we carry on lookin'.'

'Best chance of catchin' up with him might be back at the diggings,' said Blackstock. 'Leastways, it might be the best place to start.'

'I don't like goin' back,' answered Creed. 'I figure

we'll push on, see what we can find. He might still be someplace around, pannin' for gold. I figure there must be other trails leadin' down from the mountain he might have took.'

Polly looked up at him and he could see, in the firelight, that already her misery had lifted. His words had given her fresh encouragement.

'Well, whatever you do, we wish you both well. We sure thank you for savin' our skins,' said Blackstock. 'Who knows, maybe there'll be somethin' we can do to repay you one day.'

Next morning Creed and Polly bade their farewells to the prospectors and rode away, following the line of Gaunt's Peak. After a time a trail cut in from the right and they followed it as it led in a winding down-hill direction. It was very quiet with just the hushed hoofbeats of their horses and the creak of their saddles breaking the silence of the high peaks. The downward trail was steep at first, with occasional detours and switchbacks, but after a time it became easier, descending from bench to bench. They came to a high valley with towering rock walls surrounding it and, as they came closer, they saw the mouth of a canyon.

'I reckon that should lead us down to the foothills,' said Creed.

They stopped to rest and eat before riding into the canyon. Creed was watching closely for any sign indicating that riders, either singly or alone, had passed that way, but he could see nothing. Snow had drifted over the ground, making it difficult to detect any sign. Eventually they came to a branch canyon and since it seemed to lead in the direction they wanted, they decided to follow it.

The going became steep and Creed was impressed by the way Polly rode. She was obviously used to a horse and was a good rider. Behind them the great mass of Gaunt's Peak still dominated the skyline but, as the canyon began to open out, they could see that they were emerging from the high country and reaching the easier ground of the foothills.

Although they were tired they continued to ride till darkness had begun to shroud the land. They had left the mountains behind them without incident. It was time to make camp for the night. When they had built a fire, eaten and made themselves comfortable, Creed built himself a smoke.

'We didn't see any trace of those outlaws,' he said, 'but they're up there somewhere.'

'I hope those men get safely back to the diggings,' Polly replied.

'They'll be OK,' he answered. They sat in silence for a while before Polly brought up the subject which was really concerning her.

'There was no indication that my father came this way either,' she said. 'What do you think we should do next?'

Creed inhaled deeply. He had been considering the matter as they came down from the mountains.

'This is how I figure it,' he said. 'We reckoned your father might have made his way to Gaunt's Peak. He wasn't there. I figure the next best chance is back at Tamarack Creek. Maybe he headed that way after all.'

'And if he's not there?'

'If he's not there we might be able to pick up some sort of clue.'

'He could be miles away,' said Polly.

'If he's moved on he would probably have gone through Tamarack Creek. He would have needed to pick up supplies. But I don't reckon he's too far away. He came a long way to get here. I think it's more likely he would stay in the area, maybe try to stake a new claim.'

'It's not much to go on.'

'I'm open to suggestions,' Creed responded. When he got no reply he spoke again.

'If we don't have any luck, I think we should go back to the diggings. Like I say, if he's not been in town I think it likely your father is still somewhere up in those mountains. Besides, I got another idea.'

'What's that?'

'I figure things are buildin' to a showdown between the prospectors and that gang of owlhoots. I wouldn't mind bein' in at the kill. To help things along, I figure to maybe pick up a few weapons at

Tamarack Creek. Some of those boys have guns but others haven't. A few more wouldn't come amiss.'

The next morning, as he was kicking out the last traces of their fire, Creed looked back at the mountains they had left behind. They formed a line to the north and west and in the early-morning light looked almost as ethereal as the sky. He and Polly mounted up and continued their way through the foothills.

For some time Creed had noticed buzzards circling. He didn't know if they had registered with Polly. He didn't want to draw her attention to them because he knew that in her current state of mind she would jump to conclusions. They were attracted by a corpse but the chances of it being her father were, after all, slim. It was probably the carcass of a deer or an antelope.

Then, ahead of them, he perceived something that stood out on a high promontory and he knew what the buzzards were after.

'What is it?' Polly said.

'Looks to me like an Indian burial platform.'

She pulled a face.

'I think we should take a look,' he said.

Turning aside, they rode their horses to the top of the hill. The platform was about seven feet off the ground and overlooked the prairie below. Placed on the platform was a figure wrapped in a blanket. Creed could not make out whether the figure was male or female. They were making to leave when he became filled with curiosity to know who it was who had been left there. He could not tell why, but he suddenly felt that he had to know. At the same time he felt a sense of apprehension that he would be somehow violating something sacred, committing a sacrilege.

'Wait here,' he said.

He dropped to the ground and, with an intake of breath, climbed up the platform sufficiently to be able to lift the blanket and peer at the body beneath. He gave a start. The face was still recognizable as that of a young woman. Creed looked down and saw a gaping wound to her chest. It was an exit wound. She had been shot in the back.

Creed felt something close to shock. Who could be responsible for this? The gunshot wound indicated that it was probably a white man who had killed her. After carefully replacing the blanket Creed dropped to the ground. He felt shaken and he didn't know why. He had seen dead bodies before. For a few moments he stood there, then he walked back to where Polly waited and climbed back into the saddle.

'Who is it?' Polly asked.

'It's an Indian lady. She's been shot.'

Glancing at Polly, he could not help but see the look of relief on her face. Even the fact that it was an Indian burial platform had not been enough to relieve her of her anxiety. Before riding off he looked back once more at the grim outline of the platform etched sharply against the sky.

CHAPTER FOUR

After the bracing cold of the mountains it seemed strangely mild on the plains. Creed was keen to push on and reach Tamarack Creek at the earliest opportunity. In addition to the need to get back to the diggings before the bad weather set in, and before the outlaws gathering in the mountains had time to augment their numbers further, there was now the added threat from the Sioux. If he was right in his surmise that the Indian woman had been killed by whites, he and Polly were now likely to be a target.

That would put them in a strange position. He had no quarrel with the Sioux; in fact if the woman had been killed by the same outlaws as had threatened the prospectors, he was on their side. But the Sioux would be unlikely to see it that way. As he thought about it, the more convinced he became that it was indeed the same gang who were responsible. Taken together with what the Sioux had been trying to tell

him, it made sense. As Timber Wolf had said, a
pattern was beginning to emerge.

Creed had heard of similar instances before.
Outlaws were riding the owlhoot trail to the safety of
the mountains and gathering there in numbers. It
seemed they might be using the mountain fastnesses
as bases from which not just to attack the prospectors, but to raid and harass the Sioux as well. Maybe
they would even get as far as Tamarack Creek. It was
a long ride, but not beyond possibility. If that were so
they might have to contend with roving bands of
outlaws, as well as the Sioux. It was a mess and the
sooner he got Polly to the safety of Tamarack Creek
the better it would be.

Creed had observed copious sign of buffalo; now,
as they topped a slight rise, he saw a herd of the
shaggy creatures spread across the prairie. The main
body of the herd seemed to be off to their left, but
soon they were riding among bunches of them,
hispid and huge. The beasts seemed restless at their
approach, pawing the earth and lifting their heads to
sniff at the breeze. Their horns flashed in the sun.
The air was heavy with their smell and clouds of dust
and flies rose into the air.

Creed assured Polly that they had nothing to fear
from the beasts, but she was nervous. Under different circumstances Creed would have enjoyed a spot
of shooting, but, intent as he was to reach his desti-
nation, he passed them by. He figured, however, that

where there were buffalo there would also be Sioux.

That night as they lay in camp a distant, ghostly howl rose on the chilly air.

'Wolf,' Creed said to Polly.

He began to think about the creature out there in the darkness. A lone wolf. Not unlike the way he used to be. He looked down at Polly and smiled. She smiled back in return and laid her head against his chest.

'I'm glad you're here,' she said.

'I'm glad too,' he replied.

'Do you mean that?'

'Of course. Why wouldn't I?'

'I never expected—' she began, but he interrupted her.

'Neither did I.' Putting his hand under her chin, he tilted her head and they kissed.

'You know,' she whispered, 'I've been thinking about that poor Indian woman. That howl made me imagine it was her ghost out there, seeking its home. Why does life have to be so sad?'

'I don't feel sad,' Creed said. 'I feel happy that I met you. Life isn't always that way.'

She settled back in his arms. He had built a fire of buffalo chips and they were warm and comfortable. He had thought twice about the fire, but if the Sioux wanted to find them, they would do so anyway. The moon hung low and yellow, casting an eerie glow.

The wind blew from nowhere to nowhere. Then, from away across the prairie, came another sound, like distant thunder. Polly sat up and in the firelight he could see the alarm on her face.

'What was that?' she breathed.

Clouds had gathered and at first Creed thought it really was thunder, but it was too steady, too insistent. Then then he realized what it was: not thunder but drums. Somewhere, not too far away, the Sioux were dancing their war dances. He had been right about the buffalo. There was no point in trying to delude Polly.

'Drums,' he said. 'The Sioux are out there.'

The regular pulse of the drums carried over the vast silent spaces of the plains, primitive and threatening. Creed found that Polly was trembling when he took her back in his arms.

'It'll be all right,' he said. He glanced up at the Big Dipper. He knew that the Indians' favourite hour of attack was just before dawn. 'Even if the Sioux are on the warpath,' he continued, 'it doesn't concern us. Their target is the outlaws. They won't be bothered about anybody else.'

'How can you be sure of that? They might not be in a mood to discriminate.'

He drew her closer to him; for a while they were both silent but he was thinking hard. He had no quarrel with the Sioux. Really, vis-à-vis the outlaws, they were on the same side. He also realized that before they reached Tamarack Creek they would almost certainly encounter the Sioux. In order to avoid any misunderstandings, it might be wise to settle things with them if he could. Despite the obvious dangers, he could not avoid the feeling that he needed to put their relations on an amicable footing.

He remembered his brief encounter with the Sioux chief, and the warning he had been given. He would be coming back this way, perhaps with a wagonful of arms. Life would be easier if he could fix things so that he did not have to worry about the Sioux. Suddenly his thoughts were interrupted by Polly.

'What are you thinking about?' she asked. He hesitated for a moment, unsure what to say.

'I'm thinking about the best way to deal with the situation,' he replied at last.

'You mean the Sioux?'

'Yes. We have no quarrel with them. In fact, it was one of their chiefs who warned me about the outlaws.' He paused.

'Yes. Go on.'

'Well, it seems to me it might be an idea if I make an approach before there's any chance of them getting the wrong impression about us.'

'What do you mean?'

'They can't be far away. I figured on maybe riding into their camp and establishing friendly relations.'

She had been disturbed by the war drums and he was expecting an awkward reaction, but it didn't come. Instead she seemed calm. After taking a little time to consider his suggestion she looked up at him and smiled.

'I think you're right,' she told him. 'In fact, I don't see what else we can do.'

'Of course, I wouldn't put you in any danger,' he said. 'We'll find somewhere where you can stay out of sight. I'll get back just as quick as I can.'

She shook her head.

'Oh no,' she replied. 'If you go, I'm coming right with you.'

He was taken aback. He hadn't reckoned on taking her with him, but when he began to expostulate, she put her finger on his mouth.

'There's no point in arguing,' she said. 'We're in this together. I admit I was frightened at first, but I'm perfectly calm now. We've already faced dangers and come out on top. Well, this will be just one more.'

Next day they came upon the Sioux encampment. Cresting a rise, they saw their tepees beside a stream. Creed looked at Polly.

'Are you sure about this?' he said. 'There's still time to change your mind.'

She turned to him from looking down on the scene.

'I'm sure,' she replied. She smiled and, after a

moment, he returned it.

Then they touched their spurs to their horses' flanks and pressed forward. He guessed that Sioux scouts would have picked up their trail anyway. Still, he could not help a flutter of apprehension in his stomach and he could only admire the bravery and resolve with which Polly was facing the situation.

The Indian camp was still some distance away, but a group of riders had come out to meet them. Despite the cold some of them were naked but for their breechcloths and moccasins while others wore leggings and buckskin shirts. One man who appeared to be the leader wore a beaded vest. Their faces were painted and they wore feathers.

Creed looked steadily ahead as they approached, then he stopped and raised his right arm, holding it palm outwards as he had done on the previous occasion. It was meant as a gesture of friendship, but he didn't know how the Indians might react. Two of them had ridden forward. At first they made no response, then one of them held out his hand in a similar gesture. Creed observed that both Indians wore notched eagle feathers, indicating the number of enemies they had slain.

For what seemed to Creed a long time, but which was really only a matter of moments, the two parties observed each other. Despite the open palm gestures, there was tension in the air and the Sioux were regarding Polly with puzzled expressions. Creed did not want to be the first to break the silence and it was clear that the Indians were testing him out. At last Creed spoke.

'We come in peace,' he said.

The Indians continued to stare at them, then one of them replied:

'Hand over your guns.'

Creed was surprised that the man seemed to understand English. He unbuckled his gunbelt and, being careful to hold it out in front of him, handed it to the Indian.

'Come!' the man commanded: to back up his words the two of them closed up on Creed's pony.

They began to move towards the village, the other Indians falling in behind them. As they got nearer groups of women and children came out to observe their passing. The women wore long deerskin dresses and some carried babies in cradleboards on their backs. Most wore their hair in long braids, but Creed observed that some had cut it short to indicate mourning. One or two of them appeared to hurl invectives at him. He thought of the burial platform and the warning he had been given by the Indian chief. It seemed that the gang of outlaws had Sioux blood on their hands.

Dogs barked and snarled as the horses went past. The village itself consisted of about sixty buffalo-hide tepees arranged in two concentric circles. Beyond the village and closer to the stream Creed could see pony herds scattered about in groups.

Creed and Polly were escorted through the outer circle of tents to a larger tepee in the inner circle. It stood taller than the others and had a broader circumference. The outside was decorated with pictographs at whose meaning Creed could only guess. A plume of smoke rose from flaps at its tip.

The two more prominent Indians jumped from their ponies and indicated to Creed that he and Polly should do the same. The pair of them did as requested; the other Indians rode away. For a considerable time the two who had brought Creed and Polly to the camp simply stood there. Creed was unfazed. He was familiar with the Indians' propensity for doing things slowly and deliberately. It was a kind of social convention with them.

The women and children had fallen back and watched from a little distance. There were one or two old men among them but no braves. There was an oppressive atmosphere in the village. Flies droned and there was a smell of horseflesh, offal and dirt. Smoke from other tepees carried the odour of buffalo chips. Now and again a murmur of voices could be heard from inside the big tent.

Presently the entrance to the tepee opened and two figures emerged. The first one was rather startling. To begin with Creed could not make out what it was because it was almost covered by a threadbare and evil-smelling robe of animal skin which Creed

assumed was buffalo although it looked more like
bear. In one hand the figure carried a spear with a
very wide blade from which hung a variety of
coloured fringes and tassels. In the other it held what
looked like a tambourine. The figure seemed to be
walking on all fours, but then Creed realized it was a
hunchback, an old man bent like a gnarled tree on
an exposed windy slope.

Polly flinched, and so strange and unexpected was
this apparition that Creed hardly noticed the other
man who accompanied it, although he too was an
arresting figure in his own way. He was comparatively
tall and his bare upper body was strong and muscu-
lar. His face was high-cheeked and broad-browed,
and on his head he wore a full war bonnet of eagle
feathers.

When Creed eventually shifted his gaze from the
hunchback he hesitated for a moment, trying to
think where he had seen that face before; then he
recognized him as the chief with whom he had con-
versed in sign language and who had first warned
him about the potential danger from the outlaws.
The Sioux had been right. The danger had material-
ized on that mountain trail. He and Polly had been
lucky to come through it unscathed. The presence of
the man was somehow reassuring.

For long moments the two of them observed one
another. Then the chief, for so he seemed to be,
made a gesture towards the Indian who had spoken

English. The Indian approached and the chief said something to him. The man turned to Creed.

'The girl will be safe. She will be looked after till we are finished.'

At the same moment an attendant appeared, accompanied by an older woman who took Polly by the arm.

'Don't worry,' Creed assured her. 'Go with them. I will come for you soon.'

Polly did not look too happy but she allowed herself to be escorted to another tent. When she had gone the Sioux chief said something more to his lieutenant, who then turned to Creed.

'Akecheta asks why you come among his people.'

'I have no quarrel with the Sioux. I come in order to avoid misunderstanding. Blood has been spilt unnecessarily, but your enemy is my enemy.' Creed was thinking of the woman they had found on the funeral platform.

The Indian turned and spoke to the chief. The chief seemed to consider his words before replying.

'Akecheta says you are either very brave or very foolish to come to the village of his people. Either way, you need not fear. You will not be harmed.'

'Tell the chief I am not afraid, but I desire that there be friendship between us.'

Again the Indian translated. This time the chief pondered for a long time. During the course of his meditation the shrivelled figure in the animal skin spoke to him but the chief seemed to wave him aside. Creed had come to the conclusion that he was some kind of medicine man.

Finally the chief spoke to the Indian, who repeated his words to Creed in accented English.

'Akecheta invites you to step inside his tepee and talk further.'

Creed acknowledged this with a nod of the head, which needed no translation. The Indian stepped forward and with a sweep of the hand held open the entrance to the tepee. Akecheta turned and, bowing down, went inside followed by the medicine man. Creed followed and the Indian brought up the rear.

The interior of the tepee was dark after the bright light outside and at first it was difficult for Creed to make out anything clearly. As his eyes adjusted to the gloom he saw that there was a fire burning in the centre of the tepee, the smoke rising in a thin column towards the hole that served as a vent in the roof. Around the fire a few figures were seated but Creed could see no sign of the medicine man. Presumably he had taken his seat in one of the darker corners of the tepee. The seated figures adjusted their positions to make way for the newcomers, and Creed found himself sitting on a mat of rushes opposite the chief and next to the Indian who acted as translator. Creed wondered where he had learned his English.

Feeling awkward, Creed wasn't sure where to place

his legs. He took an opportunity to observe his neighbours. They were sitting cross-legged so he took his cue from them and did likewise. He looked about him and was now able to observe some objects suspended from the poles of the tepee: shields, quivers, pouches, medicine bags and buffalo masks. Creed guessed that these last were kept for ritual purposes by the men in the tepee. They made a fearsome group, their faces painted and their chests scarred. They seemed entirely uninterested in the new arrival. Their eyes were blank and impenetrable, their lips thin and tight.

The silence continued. Presently one of the Indians rose gracefully to his feet and left the tepee. He returned some moments later with an object in his hand, which he passed to the chief. Creed saw that it was a pipe, the stem of which was about two feet long, elaborately decorated and adorned with white feathers. Slowly and deliberately the chief lit the pipe from the fire. Still nothing was said. Then, holding the pipe lengthwise in his two hands, the chief looked up and began to intone some words, after which he very carefully placed the stem of the pipe in his mouth and inhaled. He held the smoke in for some moments before passing the pipe to the person sitting at his right, after which the whole process was repeated. The atmosphere in the tepee became quite close as the pipe was handed round the group, arriving in due course at Creed.

Taking what he had observed as his example, Creed drew in some smoke before handing on the pipe. The smoke was acrid and burnt his throat. When the pipe had been passed all the way round the group and had arrived back at the chief, he held it up again and spoke a few words. The Indian who was acting as translator turned slightly and addressed himself to Creed.

'Akecheta ask name.'

'Creed. My name is John Creed.'

The chief spoke again and again his words were translated.

'Now name Ohitekah. It mean brave man, warrior. Let there be friendship between Akecheta and Ohitekah, between Ohitekah and Lakota people.'

The chief placed the pipe in his mouth again and inhaled deeply. Across the narrow space he passed the pipe directly to Creed, who did the same. Then the pipe was passed round once more. When it had travelled the circle, Creed spoke.

'Tell the chief that Ohitekah apologizes for actions of bad men. Those men are beyond the law. Ohitekah wages war against outlaws. Let Akecheta and Ohitekah be united against bad men.'

His words were translated. The chief raised his hand.

'Let it be,' he said.

When Creed emerged from the tepee his eyes were at first dazzled by the bright sunlight. The groups of women and children who had followed him into the Indian camp had dispersed. In front of other tepees women were busily at work, dressing robes and drying meat. He was relieved to see Polly approaching in the company of the woman who had led her away.

In a few moments Polly's horse, together with another one, were brought up. It had been saddled and bridled and as he took the reins Creed observed that on its neck there was an image of a warpainted hand like the one he had seen on the chief's horse. An Indian brave also carried Creed's gunbelt and revolvers. The chief spoke. His words were translated.

'Akecheta and Ohitekah friends. Ohitekah keep horse. It is good horse. Go in peace.'

They mounted and made their slow way through the circle of tents. Creed turned once to observe the group standing outside the tepee and raised his hand in salute. Among them he now saw the bent figure of the medicine man, whom he had not noticed during the ceremony. Maybe it was because the ceremony had been one of peace and the medicine man's presence was only required for rituals of war.

In his mind he saw again the dead woman on the burial platform and a question suddenly occurred to him. Had she belonged to the Sioux chief? There was no way of knowing but the elaborate nature of the arrangement suggested it might be so. Akecheta had given no indication of grief but he was unlikely to display any emotion.

Whatever the truth of the matter, Creed seemed to have accomplished what he had set out to do. Perhaps he had done more. He felt good about his new-found friendship with Akecheta and the understanding he had established with the Sioux. Now it remained for him and Polly to proceed as quickly as possible to Tamarack Creek. There were weapons to be purchased. And who could tell? Maybe they'd find Polly's father, or at least pick up some information as to his whereabouts.

From his robber's roost hideout high in the mountains Dan Chantry looked out over the little, closed-in valley that was the outlaws' refuge. He was sitting on the veranda of a small, roughly built cabin. Around it were other shacks and a few tents. There was only one trail into the valley and nobody knew about it but the gunnies who had established themselves there. From one of the tents a man emerged. Running his fingers through his wiry hair, he glanced at Chantry and then came up the little slope on which the cabin had been built. It was early in the morning and the other outlaws were not yet astir.

'Plumb cold to be sittin' outside,' the man said.

'I got used to it at that minin' camp,' Chantry replied.

'Wonder how our friends are gettin' on back in

the tunnel?' the man said. 'Figure they must be gettin' mighty hungry and thirsty just about now.'

They both laughed.

'That was a lot of fun for the boys,' the man said, 'but they're wonderin' when we're gonna hit the main diggings.'

'Regan,' Chantry replied, 'you know how it is. I spent enough time there to know how much gold has been found, where it's stored and what the prospects are of us gettin' it.'

'Yeah? And what conclusion have you drawn?'

'That there ain't no future bein' a prospector.'

They both laughed again as Chantry got to his feet and walked up and down the veranda. When he turned back to Regan there was still a broad smile on his face.

'The other conclusion I've drawn is that the time to hit those prairie dogs is just about right now. And I tell you somethin' else I picked up at that goddamned mining camp. I reckon they've just about hit the mother lode.'

'That's why you were prepared to blow up the tunnel?' Regan said questioningly. 'Hell! You knew it wouldn't be there.' His face lit up and he let out a whoop.

'You'll be disturbin' the rest of the boys,' Chantry said. 'The devil knows, they need their beauty sleep.' He stopped and considered for a moment. 'They've been gettin' restless,' he said. 'Some of 'em been strayin' into Sioux territory. I don't like Injuns any more than the next man, but I figure it don't help to get them riled. And I didn't like what they did to that squaw woman.'

'Why should you worry about a little thing like that?' asked Regan. 'Anyway, them ridin' out can't do any real harm and it gives 'em a chance to let off a little steam. When you gonna tell 'em the good news?'

'I figure today would be as good a time as any.'

Regan whooped again. 'Since you been doin' all this figurin, are you aimin' to use some more of that dynamite?'

Chantry grinned. 'I reckon it might come in useful. Kind of appropriate usin' their own powder against them, don't you think?'

'I want to throw the first bomb,' Regan replied.

'You'll be gettin' a taste for it.'

As the man moved away Chantry sank into his seat again. The sun was rising above the high peaks and spilling a golden light across the far side of the valley. For a moment his thoughts turned to his daughter, who was studying at a college back East. It cost quite a bit to pay for her education. He needed money fast. After this episode maybe he would think of going straight again.

Maybe he would take a trip East to see her. But the words he had spoken to Regan, he realized, could also be applied to himself. He was getting a taste for the owlhoot life. Or yet again, with his range companion Snyder now acting as marshal at Tamarack Creek, maybe the time had come to settle down in the place where he had first stepped outside the law. After all, things were different now and with the loot he would gather as his share of the attack on the diggings, he could establish himself as a respectable citizen. There were choices, but it was good to have options.

He pulled a cigar out of his top pocket and lit it. Puffing luxuriously, he settled down to think about things in more detail, beginning with the best way, based on the detailed information he had been able to pick up during his time at the diggings, to go about relieving those prospectors of their gold.

When Creed and Polly arrived at Tamarack Creek they checked their horses at the livery stable before making their way to the Groundhog Hotel, where each of them had stayed previously before they had known one another. They waited at the desk while the clerk went to fetch the register.

'Two rooms,' Creed said.

Polly touched his arm. 'For now,' she said, smiling.

He booked for just one night. It didn't give them long to enquire about Polly's father, but he was anxious to get back to the diggings. Leaving Polly to rest in her room, he made his way to the saloon. He figured it might be as good a place as any to start asking questions.

As soon as Creed had come through the batwings and taken his place at the counter he knew there was trouble in the offing. Some men were standing at the bar. He ordered a whiskey and, as he lifted his glass, one of them half-turned in his direction.

'Injun lover.'

Creed looked in the bar mirror. He was up against three mean-looking *hombres* and they were spoiling for a fight. Even a brief glance told him they had probably been drinking for some time. That was to his advantage.

'I said, Injun lover.'

People were taking notice now and some of the men at the bar began to edge away. The piano player ceased playing. Almost imperceptibly, Creed moved his head and the barman walked very slowly towards the end of the bar.

'Looks like he ain't denyin' it,' one of the men said. The others began to laugh.

'I said you're a dirty, low-down, stinkin' Injun lover.'

Creed slowly placed the whiskey glass on the bar counter.

'Maybe he don't hear too well,' one of the gunmen remarked.

'Maybe he's a coward as well as a stinkin' Injun lover.'

There was no reaction from Creed. He was observing the position of the gunmen. They were beginning to spread out. The leader's hand was close to his gun, which he wore on his left hip, necessitating a cross draw. That would slow him down for the fraction of time that Creed might require to deal with the other two. He had seen the bead of sweat on the face of one of them. The man's hand was hovering close to his holster. He would be the first to shoot.

Having made his plan, Creed turned to face the trio.

'So you ain't deaf after all,' the gunslinger quipped.

Creed looked closely at him, watching the gunman's eyes, waiting for a flicker.

'I seen that pinto hitched outside.'

Creed said nothing.

'That's an Injun hoss.'

The man was beginning to run out of things to say. Creed held his gaze steadily. The man licked his lips.

From behind Creed someone coughed and at the same moment the man with the beads of sweat went for his gun. Before he had drawn it from its holster Creed's Colt was spitting lead and the man went down, blood spurting from his chest. Creed swung and fired at the second gunman, the shot taking him in the throat as the gunman's own gun fired harmlessly into the ceiling. Down he went too, blood pouring in pulsing spurts from his wound.

Without hesitation Creed flung himself forward as the leader's gun barked. The bullet whistled close by and went ricocheting round the saloon. Creed hit the ground and, pausing for just long enough to steady his aim, fired twice more. The man went reeling back against the bar, crashed into it and then slithered to the floor. His eyes met Creed's as both men lay on the floor, then they rolled back in his head.

Creed was on his feet in an instant, ready for action, but there was no further response from the gunslicks. Only one of them remained alive: the outlaw who had been shot in the throat. Blood was pouring from his mouth and he was making a strange gurgling noise. Then his head sank back and he was dead too.

Creed looked around him. Through the billowing smoke he could see the look of shock and disbelief on the customers' faces. They could scarcely credit the speed with which the whole incident had taken place. Then the piano began to tinkle as the piano player nervously ran his fingers over the keys. People began to talk and the barman's head appeared above the bar behind which he had taken shelter.

Then, as if he had learned of the events by thought transference, the batwings swung open and the undertaker appeared. Creed flung some dollar bills on the bar.

'That should pay for any damage. I guess the marshal will be across soon. Tell him he can reach me at the Groundhog hotel.'

He moved away, made his exit through the batwing doors and walked down the main street. His route led him past the stagecoach depot. It was where he had picked up the mail that first morning, and the old-timer was leaning back in a cane chair on the veranda.

'You owe me one hundred dollars,' Creed said.

The oldster looked at him closely and then spat.

'Goshdurn it,' he said. 'I never expected to see you again.'

'Mail's delivered,' Creed replied. 'You owe me.'

'Now just hold it right there,' the man replied. He seemed to be searching for some excuse to get out of paying but, for whatever reason, he apparently thought better of it.

'I like you, son,' he cackled. 'Remind me of myself when I was your age.'

He rocked the chair forward so that it settled all its legs on the veranda, got to his feet and walked inside the building. A few minutes later he came back out, carrying a small roll of dollars fastened with a band.

'This'll have to do on account,' he said.

Creed took the money without counting it. 'I'll be heading back to the diggings soon,' he said. 'If you got some more letters I could take them along.'

The oldster laughed once more. 'Might be something coming in on the next stage,' he said.

'When's that due?' Creed asked.

'Should be right along tomorrow noon.'

Creed nodded. 'I'll call back if I'm still around.'

The oldster watched as Creed walked away. He took a piece of cigar from his pocket and put it in his mouth without lighting it.

'Thought I heard me some shooting down towards the saloon,' he said to himself. 'Now I wonder if that boy had anything to do with it.'

CHAPTER FIVE

Creed made his way to the gun store. He had a big order. The storekeeper looked at him in surprise.

'You thinkin' about starting your own private war?' he asked.

'Somethin' like,' Creed replied.

'That's a lot of artillery,' the man said.

Creed checked the list he had drawn up. As he was doing so the door opened and the marshal came in. He was big and burly and wore a bedraggled walrus moustache.

'What's the name, boy?' he said.

'Creed. John Creed.'

The marshal scrutinized him closely.

'You seem to be mighty fast with a gun,' he said.

Creed shrugged.

'I could run you into jail right now,' the marshal continued.

Creed remained silent.

'Three men dead over in the saloon and from what I can tell you ain't been in town longer than it takes a raccoon to shake its tail.'

Creed looked the marshal squarely in the eye.

'I didn't start it,' he said. 'Those *hombres* were just looking for trouble. Ask the barman. Ask anybody at the saloon.'

'I already did,' the marshal said. He walked over to the counter and said something to the storekeeper before turning back to Creed.

'Like to tell me what you're doing?' he asked.

Creed thought for a moment. He could see no reason not tell the marshal the truth, or something close to it.

'I've been commissioned to deliver some weaponry to the diggings,' he said. 'They reckon they might be needed if they ever hit the mother lode.'

'Now that might be right or it might not,' the marshal said. 'On the other hand, maybe you're aimin' to stir up a little Indian trouble. Maybe you got some different clients. Maybe you're an Injun lover after all.' He paused, looking to Creed for some reaction, but there was none.

'This is a quiet town,' he continued. 'Leastways, it was before you arrived. I'm not sure I altogether like you. I'll give you till noon tomorrow. If you're not out of town by then, I'm going to put you in a cell.'

'I got some mail to collect,' Creed replied, 'but I don't intend stayin' longer.'

The marshal turned. As he did so Creed thought to ask one more question.

'By the way, you wouldn't know anything about a feller called Chantry, Dan Chantry?'

The marshal stopped dead in his tracks. For a moment he stood still with his back to Creed; then he turned round. There was a grim look on his face.

'Chantry?' he said.

'Yeah. Seems like he was workin' up at the diggings but he went missin'. I figured maybe he came by this way.'

The marshal affected to be thinking about the matter. The expression on his features had changed to one of puzzlement, but the grimness remained and Creed could tell he was putting on an act.

'Nope,' the marshal answered, 'can't say as I've heard of anyone called Chantry.'

'Oh well, it was only a chance,' Creed replied. He turned to the storekeeper.

'Have these items ready for me tomorrow morning,' he said. 'I'll be by to collect them.'

He turned on his heel, keen to escape the marshal's attentions. It was clear that he had touched the marshal on a raw nerve. If the lawman already had inclinations to throw Creed into jail it might be best to avoid any further dialogue. But why was the marshal so put out? He made his way back to the livery stables, where the ostler had stabled his and Polly's horses.

'Know where I can find a wagon?' he asked.

'You can get one right here,' the ostler replied.

He was a lean, weathered individual and Creed liked the look of him. He took Creed to a yard at the back of the building. In a corner stood a rather battered wagon. It didn't amount to much but it would do.

'Reckon you can fix me with a team of horses to go with it?' Creed asked.

The man thought for a moment.

'It'll cost you,' he said.

'No problem,' Creed replied. 'Have the rig ready for noon tomorrow.'

He peeled some dollar bills from the bundle in his shirt pocket.

'Pleasure to do business,' the ostler replied.

That evening Creed and Polly had a good meal in the hotel's dining salon before retiring early to Polly's room, which was on the second floor and opened on to a gallery that ran along the outside of the building. Polly was feeling tired and lay down on the bed. Taking up a position overlooking the street, Creed sat down on the gallery to watch events. Apart from the sounds of voices and a piano from the Blue Nugget saloon, things were quiet. A couple of horsemen rode up to the saloon and tied their horses to the hitch rail. A few people strolled along the boardwalks and now and again someone would enter the hotel. Creed watched them closely.

At first he had regarded the incident in the saloon as being without significance, but as he thought about it he became convinced that it was more than accidental that those three men had been there. They weren't ordinary cowboys. Their whole appearance and attitude marked them out as gunmen. If that was so, it was likely that they were members of the outlaw gang threatening the miners, or were on their way to join them.

There was a chance that there might be others in town, maybe out for revenge. This made the prospects for the journey back all the more dangerous.

Then there was the marshal. Now that some time had elapsed since their conversation, he wasn't unduly bothered about the lawman's threat to put him in jail. Still, he didn't want any complications and he had the marshal's reaction to his question about Polly's father to think about. The marshal had obviously been hiding something.

He glanced through the doorway to where he could see Polly lying on the bed. He hadn't mentioned the incident to her. It would only distract and worry her and there was nothing to be done about it. She was more exhausted than she had let on after the journey to Tamarack Creek and she would need all her strength for the return. He hoped nothing had happened up at the diggings. He had a feeling that things would work themselves out up there and he had more than a notion to be there when they did.

Creed was up and about early in the morning attending to business. Long before noon he had the wagon ready and the horses and mules prepared. As he emerged from the livery stable he saw the marshal leaning against a post, observing him closely. Creed acknowledged him with a slight touch to his Stetson.

He did not go to the saloon but instead met Polly and they took mugs of coffee with some flapjacks at a café. Sitting at a table and watching the marshal through the window, Creed tried to figure out the situation. The marshal certainly seemed to have taken an objection to him and appeared to be doing mighty little about the lawless element in town.

Creed was on surer ground about the men who had set upon him in the saloon. They were gunslicks, he was certain of it, and he was almost as sure that they were connected with the outlaws who were making their headquarters in the mountains. Was the marshal in their pay, or at least willing to turn a blind eye? There must be a whole lot of owlhoots gathering up there. They were beginning to cover a lot of territory.

He finished the last of his coffee and strode out into the sunlight with Polly. They bent their steps in the direction of the livery stable. His wagon stood full-rigged under the watchful eye of the ostler with his and Polly's horses attached at the back.

'Got her ready?' Creed enquired.

'No problems.'

Creed peeled off some more notes and gave them to the ostler.

'Mighty generous of you,' the man said.

Creed checked the horses in the traces. 'They'll do,' he commented.

He swung up to the box seat, helped Polly up beside him, and negotiated his way out of the stable. He turned into Main Street and halted outside the gun store. He walked inside.

'You got my order all ready?' he asked.

The storekeeper eyed him with distaste.

'Got everything right here,' he replied.

'Give me a hand to load it up,' Creed said.

The boxes of rifles and ammunition were heavy and it took the two of them to swing them up on to the wagon bed. While they were busy Creed noticed that the marshal had taken up a position on the opposite side of the street. When the last box had been manoeuvred into place the lawman came strolling over.

'I thought I told you to be out of town by noon,' he said.

'Leaving right now,' Creed replied.

'I'm still not sure about you,' the marshal said. 'I've a mind to run you into jail anyway.'

'On what charge?'

The marshal thought for a moment.

'How about gun runnin' for starters?' he suggested.

Creed laughed. 'You'll remember me, won't you, Marshal?' he said, and flicked the reins.

The wagon rumbled down the dusty street. Outside the stagecoach depot there was a buzz of activity. People were arguing and a woman, obviously in a state of distress, was being comforted by another woman and a middle-aged man in a dark suit. The stagecoach had arrived but Creed could see no sign of the oldster. Telling Polly to wait, he jumped down. The old man was inside the building and looked up at Creed's approach.

'Ain't no mail,' he said.

Creed looked blankly at him.

'Seems like the stage was held up outside of town. The guard was hurt and the strongbox taken – and the mail sack.'

Creed didn't wait for further details. He went back outside, climbed up on the box seat of the wagon and cracked his whip. As the wagon pulled out he looked back, to see the marshal coming down the street, heading quickly for the depot. Creed felt grateful that the marshal now had something else to occupy him. It was time to put some distance between himself and Tamarack Creek if he didn't want to run the risk of that jailhouse.

The wagon rumbled on and soon the town was left

behind. All the time Creed was thinking about the situation and the more he pondered the more problematical it appeared. Not only was he concerned that the marshal might decide to come after them, but there was the question of the outlaws to consider. If the marshal was in their pay he might try to get word to them about Creed's purchase of the weapons.

Even if he didn't, they were still a likely target for the outlaws and, if the guns fell into their hands, the situation would be worse than ever. The outlaws would be able to use them in an attack on the prospectors.

Polly was aware of his silence but her thoughts were on her father. Creed, for his part, did not want to worry her unduly with his own concerns. As the day went by and he was thinking of finding a place to camp, his uncertainties grew. When they eventually stopped beside a stream Creed set Polly to gathering materials for a fire while he attended to the horses.

After they had eaten they both felt more relaxed. Creed built himself a smoke.

'You don't mind?' he said.

'Of course not. Why would I?'

Creed shrugged.

'It's a lovely night,' she said.

Creed nodded in agreement and inhaled.

'I think, if it weren't for everything else, I could love it out here,' Polly said.

'If you don't mind me saying so, there ain't a lot of home comforts in a mining camp.'

'I've had enough of home comforts,' she said. 'So long as I find my father, I'll be content.' She raised herself up on one elbow. 'What about you, Mr Creed?'

'I got no plans. Leastways, not beyond getting safely back to the diggings with you and the armaments. Didn't intend sticking around this long. Got sort of tangled up in the situation up there.'

'You're young,' she said. 'Same as me. Don't you feel as though you just want to have it all?'

'I'm not sure what you mean. But I feel – used to feel – like I want to be free. In any case, those mountains just suit me fine.'

She said nothing for some moments. The glow of the firelight lit up her features and put highlights and shadows in her hair.

' "Used to feel??' she said. 'You said "used to feel".'

Creed looked into her eyes.

'Things are different now,' he replied. He lifted her face to his and they kissed.

'Yes,' she murmured.

They kissed again.

'I used to think how hard everything was,' she said. 'I didn't like it at the boarding school. I didn't like being away from my father. There were so many things. Now it all seems easy.'

'It will be,' he told her. 'Once we've found your

father and we've sorted out this business with the outlaws.'

She did not reply but lay curled up in his arms. Later, as she lay sleeping and he looked up at the stars, he began to reflect that it might not be so easy to find Dan Chantry. It would not even be easy just making the rest of their way back to the diggings. Perhaps he could expect an attack from the outlaws soon. If so, where would it happen?

There were a few reasons why he decided that, if it came, it would come in the high country. Most of the outlaws were up there already. The terrain offered plenty of opportunities for an ambush and, by then, he would have covered the best part of the journey, almost providing a personal delivery service with the weapons. Especially if the marshal had got a message through.

Creed was wrong. The outlaws struck early the next afternoon, a bunch of them, coming over the crest of a ridge.

'Get down!' he shouted to Polly. She was confused at first, then screamed when she saw the riders heading towards them.

'Get down in the wagon,' he shouted again. As she scrambled to shelter among the ammunition boxes he whipped up the horses. The wagon lurched forward and picked up speed. For a moment or two it seemed to keep its distance from its pursuers, but the weight of its contents began to tell as the horses strained against the traces. Creed's whip lashed out again.

Behind them shots rang out, whining overhead. Holding the reins in one hand, Creed picked up his rifle and fired off a couple of shots in return. The wagon rolled and lurched over the rough ground until suddenly, hitting some obstruction in its path, its left-hand wheels left the ground and it came crashing down on its side. The horses reared and snorted as they became entangled. Creed hit the ground with a thump, which left him winded, but he was quickly up and taking shelter behind the over-turned wagon. He looked for Polly and saw her lying among the boxes which were now scattered all over the ground. She lay on her side and was not moving; he could not tell whether she was injured.

'Polly?' he called, but she made no response. There was no time to do anything further because the outlaws were riding down fast. He grabbed his rifle, which lay near by, took aim at the nearest rider and squeezed the trigger. The horse went crashing down, crushing its rider underneath it. Creed let off another shot and a second horse tumbled head first to the ground, throwing its rider.

Shots were thudding into the wood of the wagon and ricocheting from the iron wheels. Hard-pressed though he was, Creed became aware of the danger of a shot hitting one of the ammunition boxes and setting off an explosion. He had his Colts out and was firing rapidly, but the situation appeared to be hopeless. There were at least ten of the outlaws and he could not hope to hold them off for long.

So far he had been able to prevent them from encircling him, but his guns were hot in his hands. More bullets were smashing into the wagon and pieces of splintered wood came flying down upon him. In the thick of battle he managed to glance towards the prostrate form of Polly; he detected movement.

'Stay still,' he called, realizing that her best chance was to remain where she was, even though plumes of dust raised by bullets were perilously close to where she lay. There was no way she would be able hear him through the loud crackle of gunfire.

As he ducked behind the rim of the wagon yet another bullet sang inches from his head and he realized that this was the end. He wished he had done things differently. He felt that he had betrayed his trust. What would happen to Polly? He lifted his head again and fired another shot.

Then, above the noise of battle, he heard another sound, a whooping and yelling that seemed to come from somewhere behind him. He turned his head. Through a billowing cloud of dust he saw a bunch of Sioux warriors bearing down on the scene.

The outlaws had seen them too. They loosed a few more shots, then turned their horses and galloped away. The Indians were still some way off and their fire was desultory, but even so one of the galloping outlaws flung up his arms and fell backwards as a bullet caught him in the back. The rest of them rode hard in retreat, having obviously decided not to take any further risks with the Sioux.

Creed crawled from behind the wagon to where Polly lay.

'Are you hurt?' he asked.

There was no immediate response, then she shook her head.

'What happened?' she asked.

Creed was about to reply when she caught sight of the approaching Sioux and, reaching up her arms, clung to him. In the confusion of the moment she had forgotten that the Sioux were friendly towards them.

'It's all right. . . .' Creed began to explain, then he realized that she had fainted. He got to his feet as the first of the Sioux warriors leaped from his horse and approached him. Any lingering anxieties he might have felt were put to rest as the Indian held up his hand.

'Ohitekah,' he said. 'We meet with you again.' He spoke in English.

Creed raised his palm and advanced to meet him.

'Just in time,' he said.

The rest of Sioux had dismounted and were already straining to set the wagon upright. The horses were uninjured and the Sioux leader seemed to recognize the pinto that had been given to Creed by Akecheta. Creed attended to Polly, who soon regained full consciousness. When she saw that the Sioux warriors were now standing around them she opened her mouth, but Creed gently placed his hand upon her lips.

'Friends,' he said. 'Remember, they are on our side.'

She did not seem persuaded and Creed set about trying to convince her. When she saw that they had righted the wagon and were lifting the boxes back into it she began to calm down a little. She was still quite badly shaken from the tumble but seemed to have suffered nothing more serious than a few cuts and bruises. After a time, with Creed's support, she struggled to her feet.

It was only then that both of them became aware that Creed himself had sustained an injury. There was blood flowing down his arm from a wound where a bullet had creased his shoulder.

'It's nothing,' Creed said. It was true, but it must have been a close thing. When at length things were restored to normal, the Sioux leader approached Creed.

'Bad men come back. Lakota watch for you. Guard against bad men.'

'Long way to go,' Creed said. 'Up into mountains.'

'Ohitekah brother to Lakota. His enemy our

116

enemy.' They were almost the same words as Creed had used. Creed nodded. To have the Sioux looking out for them would pretty much guarantee their safety.

The band of warriors mounted their ponies and the leader raised his arm in salute. They rode off and Creed cracked his whip. The wagon lumbered forward. Although having the eyes of the Sioux on them for the rest of the journey might have some disadvantages, Creed felt a certain relief. It offered the best chance for him to deliver both Polly and the weapons. Suddenly he found himself thinking of the mining camp and his friend, Timber Wolf Flynn. It would be good to see him again.

There was one enemy Creed had not given much thought to: that was the weather. As they climbed the foothills scurries of snow began to blow in and black clouds scudded across the skies. Creed urged the horses forward in an attempt to cover as much ground as possible. Then the weather broke, forcing them to make camp early. While Polly huddled in the shelter of an overhanging rock Creed built a lean-to of evergreen boughs and managed to find enough kindling to start a small campfire.

They drank coffee while outside the snow came down. From time to time Creed leaned forward to add sticks to the flames, while the wind blew loud and whined among the aspens and pines.

In the cold pale light of dawn Creed's eyes opened. He sat up and glanced at Polly's sleeping figure. As he did so her eyes flickered and opened. She looked at him.

'Better try to make another fire,' he said.

A flurry of wind blew into the shelter. Creed pulled on his boots and with difficulty succeeded in building a fire to make coffee. When he looked out the snow had stopped but the world was changed. A heavy blanket of white covered everything in sight and snow lay in drifts against the sides of trees, piled up.

As if by mutual agreement no words were spoken as they made their preparations and started again on the trail. In places the snow was already crusted hard and Creed had to make detours to avoid drifts. The going was slow but at least they were moving. The wind was blowing again and held the promise of more snow to come.

The day wore slowly on. They were climbing high now and snow was falling heavily. The horses were approaching exhaustion and Creed was beginning to doubt that they would make it. Polly was resting on the bed of the wagon, covered with blankets. Creed's eyes were drawn tight as he peered into the swirling void of white in front of him; from time to time he had to get down and shovel hard to clear a way for the wagon to get through. When that happened he was careful not to work up a sweat, which might freeze up inside his clothes. The wagon was barely moving.

Suddenly Creed thought he detected sounds coming from the direction of the trail ahead of him. Instantly his hand reached for his rifle. He remembered how he had been bushwhacked when coming for the first time along this trail, right by where they were now. He drew the wagon to a halt and listened carefully.

Sure enough, above the soughing of the wind and the continuous soft whispering of the falling snow, his ears picked up the sounds of muffled hoofbeats. Then a horse neighed. Creed jumped down from the wagon and moved into the brush alongside the trail. He waited, tense with anticipation. With the help of his Sioux friends he had got through this far. He didn't intend to relinquish those rifles now that he was almost back at the diggings.

Soon his eyes picked out the emerging forms of riders. There was a group of them. His thoughts leaped to Polly, lying in the wagon. He hoped she would stay where she was but there was nothing he could do about either her or the advancing horsemen except fight. Drawing a bead on the first rider, he waited. The riders continued to come forward and then Creed heard a voice say: 'Looks like there's something up ahead.'

Creed lowered his rifle. His heart leaped with relief and joy. He recognized that voice. It was

Timber Wolf Flynn.

'Timber Wolf,' he called. 'It's me. John Creed.'

He stepped out on to the snow-covered trail as the riders spurred forwards. Timber Wolf jumped from his horse and ran to seize Creed by the shoulder.

'Creed.' he shouted. 'I figured that you'd find a way back. Boy, it sure is good to see you!'

CHAPTER SIX

The mining camp lay wrapped in a threadbare blanket of snow. It had fallen almost without interruption for two days, then a thaw had set in. Neither snow nor thaw deterred the prospectors. Despite the weather, the search for gold continued. Some were still finding nuggets of gold wedged into cracks of rocks where it could be dug out with a knife. Some were following the simple method of getting traces of gold out of the sand and gravel in the streams by use of an ordinary metal bowl. Others continued to use the long tom combined with a flume and a sluice.

More and more, however, the gold seekers were tunnelling into the sides of the surrounding hills, encouraged by the discovery that the blue-black rock they had been throwing away was in fact silver ore. The gold they had been finding was light in colour because it was alloyed with that metal.

Creed and Timber Wolf, together with Polly, were

standing by the mouth of one of these tunnels, Timber Wolf seeming even huger wrapped in his buffalo coat. Polly herself seemed little the worse for all the trials and tribulations of the journey from Tamarack Creek, but she was obviously disappointed at not having found her father.

'You did a good job,' Timber Wolf said to Creed. 'We sure could use those weapons. And I don't need to tell you how grateful those boys are for you rescuin' them from that tunnel.'

'So they got back OK?'

'Sure did. And they're just itchin' to get their revenge on those renegade varmints.' He turned to Polly. 'I've been askin' around but nobody here has seen your father.'

'We'll find him,' Creed said. He turned to Polly and squeezed her.

'Once this other business is settled, we'll find him.'

The three of them remained quiet for a few moments, taking in the scene around them. Since Creed had been gone there had been some incidents. Another miner had been shot and wounded and more riders had been seen on the mountain trails, heading for wherever the outlaws had their roost. They were evidently gathering there in strength.

'Seems to me,' Creed said, 'that those varmints are fixin' to strike real soon. We'd best get prepared.

How many of the prospectors can handle a gun? The weapons need to be distributed. Those owlhoots are comin' and I don't like the idea of bein' a sittin' duck.'

Timber Wolf laughed and slapped him on the back.

'You sure are full of sand,' he said. 'Don't worry. A committee meeting's been called for tonight to organize for an attack.'

They had started to walk back downhill when White Fawn appeared, coming along a track by the side of the mountain. She was wearing a long deerskin dress over leggings and a blanket robe, and carrying a basket with some greenery in it. As she came down the track she seemed to be preoccupied, but then she noticed them and, walking lightly, came to join them.

'Herbs,' Timber Wolf said, pointing at the contents of her basket.

'Yes,' she replied, 'and as I was gathering them I saw riders. They were looking over the camp. They were a little way off and I made sure they did not see me.'

Timber Wolf turned to Creed. 'Looks like you're right,' he said. 'Things is hottin' up.'

Creed looked over the snowy camp. 'I hope we're doin' the right thing,' he said. 'These men are prospectors, miners. They didn't come here to get involved in fighting.'

'We're doin' the right thing,' Timber Wolf replied. 'Look around you. What do you see? Anything different since you left for Tamarack Creek?'

'Plenty of snow,' Creed replied.

'Look up into the side of that mountain we just come down from.'

Creed looked back. The mountain was pitted with tunnels and shafts going down into the ground.

'Seems like a heap of diggin' is going on,' Creed replied. Timber Wolf grinned.

'You're right. The reason for that is they think they've hit the mother lode. Up till now they've been finding traces of gold in the river and streams or little nuggets in the rocks. But that's just the gleanings. The gold comes from somewhere. It comes from the rock, from within the mountain, and it crops out.

'They think they're getting to the source, and that's why they've started tunnelling. They've started up there because they reckon there's an outcrop for a lode that goes right along the face of the mountain. And what that all means is that they don't intend runnin' or givin' up now they've got this far. They'll fight.'

He paused.

'They'll fight because they can see an outcome to all their efforts. And once they've fought off the gunnies they'll go on workin', because if it's true that they've found the mother lode, this place is going to be jumpin' come the spring. The veins near the surface will work out. Like I said before, they'll have to mine deeper to get the ore. But they'll do it. They'll do all that as well.'

Creed recalled some words Timber Wolf had said previously on the same subject.

'Could be profitable for you,' he said, echoing them.

'Yes, you're right. But I won't be here when that happens.'

'What will you do?'

'Sell out, move on.' He looked at Creed. 'How about you?'

'I shall move on too,' Creed said. 'Just as soon as this business with the outlaws is settled I aim to head out.' He glanced at Polly. 'We aim to head out.'

'Of course,' Timber Wolf said. 'To find Polly's father.' He stopped to reflect for a moment.

'Kinda strange in a way, ain't it?' he said. 'You and me, Creed, both fixin' to risk our lives for nothin'. At the end of the day we neither of us have any stake in what goes on here. Why don't you two just move on right now? You've already done more than enough for these folks.'

Creed shrugged. 'Guess it comes with the mail,' he said.

The following day the skies were filled with dark clouds but the snow had turned to a cold rain. The camp presented a miserable sight, where melting snow formed great puddles and the tracks were turning to mud. Higher up the snow was lying thickly and from time to time fell in little avalanches down the mountain sides.

Timber Wolf was proved right as far as the committee meeting went. Now that it seemed they had hit pay dirt, most of the men wanted the outlaws dealt with before work on digging into the mother lode started in earnest. There was an air of excitement in camp because everyone knew that something big was about to happen. They felt they were on the verge of a major breakthrough that would make all their fortunes and they were ready to face up to the threat from the outlaws.

Creed was aware of the atmosphere of subdued euphoria but he was uncertain how long it would be sustained. It made sense to tap into it while it lasted. The weapons he had brought from Tamarack Creek were distributed. A lot of the men already had guns. By the time they had finished they were a well-armed group. In the vanguard were the men Creed had saved from being buried alive and they did not hesitate to shower him with their thanks.

'We owe our lives to you,' Blackstock told Creed. 'We won't ever forget it.'

Early next morning Creed and Timber Wolf were up and about, superintending the building of defences. It seemed there were only two ways into the valley: the trail by which Creed had entered it and one other, which one of the prospectors had discovered, leading through a narrow canyon. Timber Wolf took charge of a team of men blocking off the entrance to the canyon while Creed with another group began to construct ditches and earthworks across the main trail. He didn't think they would be very effective but at least they would slow and hamper the outlaws' progress. Creed was certain that the attack was inevitable and could come at any time.

He would have liked to have some idea as to the number of the outlaws but it was impossible to estimate with any accuracy. The likelihood was that there would be plenty of them. They had had time to assemble and from the incidents which had already taken place it was reasonable to deduce that they had gathered in strength.

When the defences had been completed the prospectors were assigned positions from which to defend the camp. Some were stationed among rocks and bushes alongside the main trail and others on the roofs of shacks and cabins, from where they could get a decent overview of the settlement. Finally Creed organized a group of horsemen who could ride to whichever point of the action might need additional support.

The two women, Polly and White Fawn, were under strict instructions to remain under cover in Timber Wolf's store. When they raised objections a concession was made. They were to look after ammunition stores and carry supplies to those people charged with the defence of the store itself, which was the focal point of the diggings. Supply dumps were placed at strategic points around the camp. By mid-afternoon the men had done everything they could and were prepared to take up their positions at the first sign of hostilities.

'Let's hope it comes soon,' Creed said. 'The men have been too occupied today with the arrangements to have time to start gettin' nervous.'

'Don't worry none,' Timber Wolf barked. 'They won't let themselves down.'

Creed looked up at the surrounding hills.

'They might be up there, watchin' us,' he said.

'I don't think so,' Timber Wolf responded. 'They figure we'll be easy meat. If they'd been that concerned they'd have taken more effort to make sure you didn't get through with those guns.'

'I had the Sioux to thank for that,' Creed replied.

'Maybe they're up there watchin' too,' Timber Wolf said.

Night descended. A few of the men were still at work but activity in the camp was at a low ebb. Campfires glowed and from somewhere there came the plaintive sound of a harmonica. Otherwise the place was strangely silent. The customary hum of voices was absent and the prospectors were silent, thoughtful, their attention concentrated on what the morrow might bring.

After a time the harmonica ceased and only an occasional cough broke the stillness. Creed was sitting with Timber Wolf outside the store. Light spilled from the open doorway and lit up his grizzled features.

'Funny about Polly's father,' he remarked.

Creed's thoughts had been elsewhere. Now he turned his attention to the big man.

'How do you mean?' he asked.

Timber Wolf was smoking a corn cob pipe; he inhaled deeply before replying:

'Well, seems to me there ain't a lot of places he could be between here and Tamarack Creek and you checked most of 'em out.'

'There's a lot of country,' Creed replied.

'But not much of it a man would be headed for.'

'What are you gettin' at?'

Timber Wolf glanced over his shoulder towards the store entrance.

'You might have to face the possibility that those outlaw varmints got him,' he said. 'After all, he was a lone man and they almost did for you.'

Creed didn't reply for a moment. He suddenly realized that Timber Wolf's words had simply brought into the open something that had already occurred to him without it ever quite coming to the surface.

'It's worth thinkin' about,' Timber Wolf said. 'That

young lady of yours seems to have it pretty firmly fixed in her head that she's goin' to find her father. Maybe she will, maybe you both will. But sometime she might need to face the possibility that he's gone for good. Otherwise she could spend an awful lot of time chasin' after a shadow. That ain't a good thing to do.'

Creed looked at his friend. There was more to the big man than met the eye. He wondered what there was in Timber Wolf's past that had led him to that conclusion.

'Tell me again why they call you Timber Wolf,' he said.

Timber Wolf turned his head and glanced up at the mountains. He took a long pull on his pipe before replying:

'Truth is, I just don't know. I been called that for a long time. Guess someone somewhere just come up with it and it kinda stuck. Most of my life I been a mountain man makin' a livin' outa huntin' and trappin'. Those days are gone but, like an old timber wolf that don't know nothin' different, I've stayed on.'

He paused and looked closely at Creed. 'A wolf is a pack animal, but for a long time I was a different kind of timber wolf. Reckon you could say I was a buffalo wolf. You know what that is?'

Creed shook his head.

'A buffalo wolf is a lone wolf. He doesn't hunt with

the pack. He's on his own, sometimes for choice, sometimes by necessity. In my case I guess it was a bit of both. I thought I liked bein' on my own, standin' out apart from the rest. I used to take a pride in it; I used to figure it was a mark of distinction.'

He looked again at Creed whose face was silhouetted in the open doorway.

'Somethin' about you reminds me of myself when I was your age,' he went on. 'But you're luckier. You have someone. It took me long years of bein' a buffalo wolf to discover my mistake. That was when I found White Fawn. That was when I stopped chasin' shadows and settled for somethin' solid and real.'

'And this place?'

'This place is real enough, real enough to fight for. But it's only a place. Other places are just as good or just as bad. It depends who you're in 'em with. I guess I'm tryin' to say that I would hate to see anythin' come between you and Polly. And that includes chasin' after a chimera.'

'A what?'

'Somethin' not real. I mean her father – that is: if he's not around any more. Like I say, that's somethin' she might have to learn to accept.'

'But if he is around someplace?'

'Then you'd better find him real soon.'

At that moment a shadow fell across them and White Fawn appeared through the doorway, carrying two tin cups filled with strong black coffee.

'You spend long time talking,' she said. 'It is cold outside.' She handed the cups to them and Timber Wolf took a sip.

'That sure hits the spot,' he said. 'Be right along. We've just about finished out here.'

White Fawn went back inside. After finishing both his pipe and his coffee, Timber Wolf followed. Creed sat on for a while, sipping his drink, then he got to his feet and made his way towards the stream. Timber Wolf's words had set him thinking and were making him restless. He didn't like being presented with the sorts of difficult decisions he had had to face recently; in particular, what to do about Polly's father.

He was content to carry on the search for him but Timber Wolf was correct. They couldn't go on searching indefinitely. If they didn't find him soon they would have to give up. But could Polly be persuaded to do that? He looked about him at the dark shapes of the mountains and felt that he would almost be grateful when the attack came. At least that would be something he wouldn't have time to think about.

Early the next morning, as soon as they had eaten, the men took up their positions. Timber Wolf made his way to the canyon entrance and Creed rode along the trail leading down into the valley. He knew that some of the prospectors were lying in wait behind

trees and bushes, but he could not see them. He satisfied himself that things seemed to be in order and
then continued up to the top of the track.

Just to the right of its juncture with the main trail
leading up from the foothills there was a patch of
rocks. He slipped from the saddle and led the horse
into the shelter of some bushes; then he took up a
position behind the rocks. From whichever way the
outlaws approached, he would be able to see them
coming.

He figured to loose off some shots, make his way
through the trees to where he had left the horse, and
then be in a position to make his way back down to
the valley floor, either through the trees or, more
directly, down the track itself. The latter option
might be dangerous if the prospectors were to open
fire too rashly. He checked his guns, placed them
back in their holsters, then lay back behind the cover
of a boulder, his Paterson centre-hammer rifle alongside him, to await any possible developments.

A long time seemed to pass and Creed began to
think his plan was a bad one. After all, there was
nothing to say the outlaws were coming that day. It
could be at any time, but Creed knew it would be
soon so he decided to stay on a bit longer. A fine mist
had been lying over the valley when he set out but
the climbing sun had cleared most of it away; now he
had a clear view in either direction.

His back began to ache and he shuffled about to

find a new position. Then he stopped moving and listened intently. From somewhere near by he heard something – the snapping of a twig? – and he swung his rifle round towards the bushes. Although he could see nothing very clearly, he thought he could detect movement.

His finger was already set to pull the trigger when a figure appeared briefly in view behind a tree and he recognized White Fawn. She must have seen him because she stopped abruptly, her body frozen in an attitude of surprise. Creed lowered the rifle and beckoned to her to come forward. She had recognized him and stepped quickly towards him.

'White Fawn,' he whispered. 'What are you doing here?'

She seemed to have recovered her poise and did not appear to be flustered.

'I come to collect herbs,' she said.

'Collect herbs?' Creed gasped.

'Yes, but that not important. Bad men come this way. I return to camp to warn.'

'Bad men? They come now?'

'Yes,' she said. 'Listen.' She held her finger up to stress the need for silence. Creed strained his ears but could hear nothing.

'You not hear?' she said after a few moments. 'There are lots of them. They come from two directions.'

He listened again and this time thought he could

hear the distant drumming of horses' hoofs. The sound faded and he thought he must have been mistaken, but then it came again. Maybe the sound had been muffled by some intervening outcrop of rock.

'I see some of them,' she said. She paused awkwardly.

'How many?' Creed prompted.

'Twelve in group I saw, but that not important.'

'Not important?' Creed repeated.

White Fawn's lips had drawn together and she seemed reluctant to say more. Then she opened her mouth and looked at him with her big brown eyes.

'I see Mr Chantry ride with bad men.'

For a moment her words failed to make any impression. Creed was trying to work out what his next move should be and the name of Chantry did not register. Then a dawning look of disbelief indicated that White Fawn had struck home.

'Mr Chantry?' he said. 'You mean Polly's father?'

'Yes, Polly's father. You look for him.'

'What was he doin' ridin' with the outlaws?' Creed asked, still confused. 'Do you mean he was a prisoner?'

'No.' White Fawn shook her head. 'He ride out front. He with them.'

'How can you be sure?' Creed said. 'You didn't know Mr Chantry very well. Maybe you are mistaken? Maybe it was somebody else who looked like him?'

'I not mistaken,' she replied. 'I recognize.'

135

Creed was about to raise further questions but then desisted. He knew that White Fawn's powers of observation were to be trusted. In any event, further discussion was rendered superfluous as the sound of the approaching horsemen grew louder.

'They still some way off,' White Fawn said.

Creed could see no sign of alarm or panic and was impressed by her calm demeanour.

'What you do here?' she asked.

Creed quickly explained his plan. 'You'd better get on back to the camp,' he added.

'I stay with you.'

'No. You are unarmed and would only get in the way. Go now. Don't be concerned. I will be following close behind.'

Again she looked at him closely before almost imperceptibly nodding her head.

'You are right,' she said. 'I go warn Timber Wolf.'

She turned and began to make her way through the bushes. For a moment Creed watched her movements, then she was gone.

Taking a deep breath, he resumed his position behind the rock and looked down the trail. As White Fawn had warned, the hoofbeats appeared to becoming from both directions. It was just a question of which group of horsemen arrived first. He calculated distances. Down one trail he had a clear perspective for about thirty yards and for maybe five yards less down the other. He wiped his hands on his jeans and bent his head to listen. The hoof beats were steadily increasing in volume.

Then suddenly the surrounding silence was shattered by the booming crash of gunfire. Creed cursed under his breath. Either the gunslicks had seen someone or one of the prospectors had got jumpy and opened fire. Either way his own plan had been circumvented.

He was about to move back into the bushes when bullets began to sing around him, whining over his head and ricocheting from the boulders. He dived for the cover of his rock and, as the first rider appeared down the left-hand trail, squeezed off a shot which sent the man tumbling backwards from his horse.

Other riders were coming up close behind and Creed began to fire as rapidly as he could take aim. A horse fell and another one reared, unseating its rider. He went down with a scream as the horse's hoofs landed on his prostrate body. Behind him other horses were plunging and a couple of them were racing away back down the trail. Bullets ricocheted all around and rock fragments exploded like shells but Creed had a good position.

Having extricated themselves from the mêlée that had resulted from his first shots, the remaining gunslicks had retreated out of sight. Shots were still being fired from somewhere in their rear. Jamming shells into his rifle, Creed looked down the trail in the opposite direction. There was no sign of riders coming but a few stray shots told him that something was happening down there. He decided it was time for him to make a move.

Taking advantage of the shelter of the bushes where White Fawn had gone before him, he made his way back to where he had left his horse. He mounted and rode slowly through the trees, being careful to avoid any of the places where he knew some of the prospectors were concealed. Shooting had opened up again at the top of the trail, but it was sporadic. It seemed the outlaws were regrouping. Maybe they were waiting for the rest of their compadres to join them.

There was no proper trail through the trees and the way down was not easy. Presently the vegetation thinned and Creed had glimpses of the camp now not far below him.

Coming at an angle, he was about to emerge on to an open space when he detected something off to his left. He reined in the horse and drew out his field glasses to take a closer look. Away off towards the skyline he could see a substantial group of riders wending their way slowly down from the rim. It must be the second group of gunslicks and they seemed to have found a way down into the valley that none of the prospectors knew about.

That meant they would come in from a position behind the settlement, between where Creed had been stationed and where Timber Wolf was keeping an eye on the other entrance. They would be able to outflank the prospectors and come at them from a position where they were weakest.

Creed urged his horse back into the trees and began the final descent, keen to get back and warn the prospectors of what was happening. He would need to round up as many of them as could be spared from their posts, to go and meet the unexpected assault. Touching his spur to the pinto's flanks, he veered to his right and after a time emerged on the trail just where it reached the bottom lands and began to flatten out.

Behind him the sound of gunshots was coming thick and fast; the outlaws up there must have regrouped and started the descent into the valley. Creed rode hard, quickly covering the remaining distance between him and Timber Wolf's store. There he dropped from the saddle and ran inside.

'Any news?' one of the men asked.

'A bunch of outlaws are comin' down the trail. There's another group headed down from the rim further along. We need to round up a few men to go and meet them.'

The sound of shooting could clearly be heard, so the man didn't hesitate before moving off to do as Creed suggested. It was now that Creed realized the good sense of having a mobile group of horsemen in reserve. From the back room of the store Polly appeared, looking very concerned.

'Thank goodness you're safe,' she gasped, running to Creed. 'I was so worried.'

'I'm fine,' Creed said. 'What about White Fawn? Did she get back OK?'

Polly nodded.

'She's gone to find Timber Wolf and tell him what's happening.'

The prospector had returned and the horsemen were waiting outside.

'You stay here,' Creed said to Polly. 'Keep out of sight. You have a job to do but don't take any risks. Stay under cover.' Leaving Polly standing there, he rushed out and mounted his horse once more.

Polly remained looking out of the doorway. As Creed rode with the others, he was scanning the hills, but the trees obscured the gunslicks from sight and it was difficult to pick out the exact spot where he had seen them. Looking over to his right, he could see activity towards the area where Timber Wolf was positioned and guessed that the measures they had taken there to circumvent the outlaws had not proved sufficient.

The crash of gunfire was raging across the valley from various directions now and for the first time Creed began to have serious doubts about the prospectors' ability to hold off their attackers. The outlaws were coming from unexpected positions and there seemed to be more of them than anyone had anticipated. During the time that the outlaws had been gathering in the mountains they had probably surveyed the scene and made themselves familiar with passages into the valley that the prospectors were not aware of. If so, there was a danger that the prospectors would be overwhelmed.

Creed arrived at the point for which he was aiming and jumped from his horse. Running hard, he soon got considerably ahead of the others, who were men older than himself. He was approaching the cliff face, which seemed to offer no way down. He drew out his binoculars, scanned the cliff and saw what he had so far missed.

A little way along there was a narrow cleft in the rock wall, partly obscured by undergrowth and fallen rocks. He surmised that the trail he had seen the outlaws following came down the mountain and funnelled into the cleft, which eventually debouched on to level ground at this point.

He turned and urged the others forward before plunging on again. If they could reach the cleft before the outlaws came through they would have a good prospect of picking them off as they emerged. They would probably not be able to ride more than two abreast.

Breathing heavily, he hurtled onwards as fast as his legs would carry him, but before he could reach the spot his heart sank: he could see the first riders appearing through the gap. He ran for the shelter of some rocks, signalling the men coming behind him to take cover. Other riders began to emerge, then a shot whistled over his head in the direction of the prospectors. The riders had seen them and the first shot was followed by a further volley.

Glancing behind him, Creed saw one of the miners go tumbling over. He didn't stop to take in any more but began to fire at the outlaws, who were spreading out and beginning to move in the direction of the camp. A horse went down, flinging its rider over its head, and two other riders threw up their arms and fell backwards from their saddles. Creed wasn't sure whether his own weapon had delivered the shots or that of one of the prospectors.

He continued firing, but now he was faced with a new problem. A couple of the gunslicks must have seen him because suddenly they were riding hard down on him. He pulled the trigger of his rifle but he was out of ammunition. He flung the rifle to one side, drew his six-guns and began firing with both weapons as the horses bore down on him. One of the horsemen fell but the other kept coming on.

Creed felt a stab of pain in his shoulder and he reeled backwards, stumbling and then falling into the path of the oncoming horse. He looked up and it seemed that the animal was right upon him. He tried to roll over and succeeded in changing his position so as to miss direct contact with the flying hoofs, but not enough to avoid them altogether.

142

He felt a sickening surge of pain as one of the horse's front hoofs landed in his stomach; then the horse stumbled and fell, landing on Creed's left leg before struggling back to its feet. The rider fell off to one side and Creed awaited the shot that would finish him off. It did not come. Wincing with pain, Creed turned his head to see the outlaw lying prone in the mud. The horse had carried on running.

Creed's stomach felt as if a branding iron had been laid across it, and he was badly winded. Gasping for breath, he tried to get into a better position and was immediately sick. He managed to get to his knees, then he felt a hand on his arm.

'Creed, are you badly hurt?'

The questioner was one of the prospectors. For a few minutes Creed could not speak as he tried to catch his breath. The first flood of nausea passed off a little and he was able to look up and reply.

'I'm OK. The horse trod on me and I've taken one in the shoulder, but it don't seem too bad.'

The man took a look at the wound.

'It's bleedin' pretty bad,' he said, 'but nothin' seems to be broken.'

Creed got to his feet. Gunfire was booming all across the valley and scattered groups of men and horses could be seen in conflict. A bunch of riders seemed to have broken through in Timber Wolf's direction and Creed feared for the safety of his friend.

'Help me bandage up my shoulder,' he said.

The man took Creed's proffered bandanna and wrapped it round the wound. He took off his own bandanna and added it as a kind of extra makeshift dressing, tying it tight.

'Thanks,' Creed said. 'That should hold the bleeding.'

'The outlaws came off worse,' the man said. 'We got quite a few of 'em.'

Creed could see bodies lying on the ground as some of the prospectors came towards them.

'Let's get back to the store,' Creed replied.

A big battle seemed to be in progress there. They could see puffs of smoke billowing from the windows and some of the outlaws had taken up positions around the building. Creed and his companions moved in that direction; as they did so shots pinged all around them. They hit the ground, looking about for the direction of fire, but it was difficult to tell where it might be coming from as the whole scene had degenerated into a seething mêlée. Guns were blazing all around and the noise was deafening. Creed decided to take a chance. He got to his feet and moved forward again.

Then there came a blinding flash of light and he was struck by a blast of air that sent him to his knees. A dense cloud of smoke was rising from an area to the rear of the store where a number of outlaws had gathered. Creed was stunned but only for a moment.

He realized that a blast of dynamite had taken out a number of the outlaws attacking the store and that many of those who remained were too stunned to respond.

Seizing advantage of the confusion, he got to his feet and under cover of the dense smoke made it to the store entrance. He flung himself inside.

'Hold your fire,' someone shouted. 'It's Creed.'

He lay on the floor and the last thing he remembered before a dark mist descended was the figure of Polly bending over him. It didn't last for long. In a matter of minutes he came round to find that someone had laid him on a bed. For a moment he couldn't think where he was until a huge outburst of noise assaulted his ears and he realized the fight was continuing. He sat up and his head swam but in another moment he was on his feet and making his way through the door.

He took in the scene instantly. Men were firing through the shutters and a couple of bodies lay on the floor. Polly had a rifle in her hand and was positioned behind an aperture. She looked round as he staggered into the room.

'What are you doing?' she screamed. 'You've been wounded.'

'I could ask you the same question,' he replied. 'Give me a rifle, somebody.'

One of the men turned his head and Creed recognized Blackstock, who threw across the rifle he was holding and picked up another that was propped against the wall.

'Are you sure you're up to this?' Blackstock shouted.

'I'm up to it,' Creed replied.

Taking the place of one of the fallen prospectors, he positioned himself behind a vacant window space. He couldn't see anybody outside but there was a huge blackened crater where the dynamite had gone off. He looked at Blackstock.

'Was it you who threw the dynamite?' he called.

'Wished I had a few sticks,' Blackstock shouted back. 'Nope, it wasn't me. I figure the outlaws brought it along and somethin' went wrong. For them, that is.'

'Well, it was your dynamite. Looks like you got your revenge for what they did to you,' Creed replied.

Any further conversation was suddenly halted by another solid burst of gunfire outside. Shots thudded into the wooden frame of the building and one came though an aperture, to smash against the counter. Creed fired in return, but everyone was firing blind. A further fusillade of shots came raining in on the store.

Creed looked anxiously towards Polly. Although she hadn't done as he had asked her, he couldn't help feeling proud of her. It was typical that, seeing their numbers reduced, she had taken the place of someone else in the defence of the store. He realized there was no point in trying to stop her. He thought about how she had conducted herself throughout, from the time she had started off on her journey across hostile, unknown country in search of her father, to the moment when they had encountered the Sioux. Now this. She was quite a girl.

He turned back to his vantage point and, peering through the smoke that blanketed the area, strove to see what was happening outside, but it was no use. He needed to find somewhere that would allow him a sweeping view of the area. He thought rapidly. The only place where he might have a chance of doing so was the roof.

He called to Blackstock and outlined his plan to get up there. The shooting had died down a little and he decided to take his chance. Blackstock guided him through the storeroom to a little room at the back with a ladder leading up to a hatch.

'The trapdoor gives access to a loft,' he said. 'A sky-light opens on to the roof.'

Creed nodded and stepped on to the ladder.

'Be careful,' Blackstock said. 'There's a slope but it's fairly gradual. Trouble is there ain't anythin' in the way of a parapet.'

'I'll stay low,' Creed replied. 'The outlaws won't be expectin' anybody up there.

He quickly climbed the ladder and pushed against the trapdoor. It moved easily and he climbed through to the loft. Beams were laid across; they were quite widely spaced with yawning gaps between them. Carefully, Creed placed his weight on the first beam and stretched out his leg to reach the next one. For a moment he hesitated, then, trusting the beam to support his weight, he swung his leg across. He stood balanced on the beam, wishing there was a pole or something he could use for support.

He turned to face the next beam and stepped across again. Briefly he wobbled but, regaining his balance, he stepped across to the third beam; this placed him more or less beneath the skylight. A dusty pane of cracked glass separated him from the outside world but there was no catch. Reaching high, he smashed the glass with the butt of his six-gun. The movement caused him to wobble and as shattered glass rained down on him he wavered again and almost fell.

He swore beneath his breath, then he reached up and, exerting his muscles, pulled himself level with the opening. It was narrow but his straining arms supported him so that he was able to raise his head clear and peer around him. He could see quite a long way in front of him but it was difficult to turn round to get an overall view. Heaving himself higher, he placed his leg against the ridge of the roof and pulled himself clear of the skylight. As Blackstock had told him, the roof sloped but it was not at too sharp an angle and Creed had no fear of slipping off, even though the roof was icy and wet.

Creed raised his head and surveyed the scene below him. All around pockets of fighting were taking place and in the immediate vicinity he could see where the outlaws had taken their positions around the front of the store. He couldn't see much at the back because that was where the smoke lay thickest but, from the little shooting that was taking place there, he reckoned there were few if any of the gunslicks in that position. The ones who had positioned themselves there had probably been blown sky high by the explosion.

Around the valley lay the bodies of a considerable number of men and horses, and down by the stream he could see more bodies lying in the water. A fierce battle seemed to be taking place by some tents on the further side of the stream. Creed was annoyed with himself for not having brought his field glasses, but he didn't need them to see that the situation of the prospectors was becoming hopeless. They were clearly well outnumbered and it was only a question of time before they would be defeated. Even a fresh stock of Blackstock's dynamite would not be sufficient to wrestle the advantage away from the gunslicks; if it wasn't for the supply of weapons he had brought from Tamarack Creek they would in all likelihood have been overrun already.

He glanced up towards the summits of the peaks; there seemed to be movement high up there.

Looking closer, he thought he could see horses. He didn't wait to see more. If the outlaws were bringing up reinforcements the prospectors were well and truly doomed. He was about to clamber back through the skylight when suddenly the firing immediately below ceased. A loud voice broke the sudden stillness.

'Stop shooting and come out with your hands up. Your situation is hopeless.'

Creed stayed low as an answering voice, which he recognized as that of Blackstock, replied from the interior of the store.

'Go to hell!'

'If you need a little persuasion, I suggest you take a look through a side window.'

From down below Creed heard movement. He raised his head and through the swirling smoke he saw White Fawn standing in the open, her hands tied behind her back. For a few moments the only sounds to be heard were those of the fighting still taking place elsewhere. Creed tensed. How had White Fawn fallen into the enemy's hands and what had become of Timber Wolf?

'If you want the squaw woman to live you'd better throw aside your weapons and surrender.'

Creed drew his six-gun and slithered forward, trying to ascertain where the voice was coming from. Suddenly there came a loud cry from inside the building and the voice of Polly rose into the air.

'Father! Where are you? I can't see you.'

There was a hushed silence, then Polly emerged into the yard. She ran forward, before stopping to look around her.

'Father, it's me. It's Polly, your daughter.'

Creed tensed. He didn't understand what was going on but the two women standing out in the open were in an extremely vulnerable position. His eyes scanned the scene through the smoke, watching for the slightest sign of movement. Tension hung in the air and even the distant sounds of gunfire seemed to ease, as if the fighters there were waiting on events. The silence was eventually broken by a man's voice.

'Polly? What are you doing here?'

Creed turned his head in the direction of the voice but still he could see nothing. Then another voice rent the air.

'Chantry? What the hell is goin' on?'

'Shut up, Regan!'

'I don't know what your game is, Chantry, but you led us into this. You said it would be easy. I'd hate to think it was you set that off that explosion.'

'Polly, get back inside.' Chantry's voice called.

Creed was weighing up the options. None of them looked good for Polly or White Fawn. From what he could see of the battle generally, the owlhoots had the upper hand all round. The shooting had died down because the prospectors were beaten. Some of the outlaws were openly swaggering about, seeking their horses. Across the stream some of them had mounted and were heading this way.

Worse still, Creed could just perceive riders coming down from the heights overlooking the valley. In the direction of the canyon, other people could be seen moving about and from their midst a horse and rider broke forward, travelling at speed. Creed saw wisps of smoke, which suggested that the rider was being fired at, and a little way ahead of him a group of riders was gathered near the stream. They did not seem to notice the rider coming up fast behind them until he was amongst them, scattering them as he rode. Moments later he was splashing across the stream as the nearest of the disturbed riders set off in pursuit.

Creed stared hard, trying to make out who the rider was. The fact that the outlaws were following behind suggested to him that the rider was on his side. Then the man's hat flew off and his streaming locks told Creed that he was none other than Timber Wolf.

Any further chance of observation was ended by what was happening nearer at hand. Through the smoke Creed perceived the head of a man poking out from behind a corner of a shed just behind the store, where he had been hiding. The head was pulled back, to be replaced by the barrel of a rifle; it was aimed at Polly. Creed went cold all over and felt a tingling in his scalp.

Raising his six-gun, he took careful aim, waiting for the very instant when the man's head should reappear. Time seemed to slow down; the next few moments were like an eternity. Creed tried to bring his tembling hand under control. His position was not ideal because he had to partly twist himself to take aim at all. From the corner of his eye he could see the two women still standing in the yard.

Then time resumed with the shattering explosion of a rifle shot and the man who had been concealed behind the wall fell forward. As he did so his own rifle went off, the bang coinciding with a second shot from somewhere behind him. His head seemed to burst like a ripe grapefruit. Then a voice shouted something but the words were drowned as the whole scene burst into a cacophony of gunfire.

Creed didn't hesitate. In a matter of seconds he had slid down the sloping roof and dropped to the ground as bullets tore up the earth all about him. Ignoring the shooting, he dashed forward and seized Polly. He dragged her back towards the store building, trying to shield her as best he could.

At the same moment Timber Wolf's horse came crashing through a row of tents and, barely slackening its speed, carried on through a hail of bullets into the yard. As the horse came alongside White Fawn, Timber Wolf leaned down, put his arm around her and swept her up. Then he carried on galloping. The power in his shoulders was huge but it took every ounce of his strength to hold on to her. The horse went ploughing on and out of sight as Creed burst through the doorway of Timber Wolf's store, pushing Polly in front of him. Barely pausing, Creed seized a rifle he had left propped against the wall and began pumping lead into the yard.

'There's more of 'em comin'!' Creed shouted. 'I seen them on top of the ridge.'

'What can we do?'

Creed didn't reply. He glanced at Polly who had sunk to her knees on the floor.

'Maybe we'd better make a break for it?' Blackstock yelled.

The dressing on Creed's shoulder had come away and the wound was bleeding but he scarcely noticed it. Bullets were slamming into the walls of the building and it was by sheer luck that he had made it back inside with Polly. He was unsure what to do next; then suddenly, over the roar of gunfire, a new sound came to their ears, growing rapidly louder. It was a wild throbbing yell that sent tremors of fear running through the prospectors, but it brought a slow smile to Creed's features.

'Indians!' he yelled. 'Don't worry, they're on our side. It's the Sioux.'

He had been wrong about those mounted figures coming down from the ridge. They weren't outlaws but the Sioux warriors, with his friend Akecheta probably in the vanguard. The outlaws besieging the store had heard them too, because the barrage of gunfire suddenly died down and all became silent.

Creed moved cautiously to the door and peered out. The gunslicks had taken to their horses and were scattering in various directions. The Sioux had spread out across the valley and all around they were riding down the outlaws. Some of them had guns but most of them carried bows and a hail of arrows showered down on the retreating gunslicks. The fearsome war cries of the Indian braves rang out more loudly than ever. Individual battles were taking place where the outlaws had gathered in reasonable numbers, but it didn't look as though they presented a real threat any longer. Despite everything, Creed couldn't help a low chuckle escaping from him. Just at the point when all seemed lost they had been saved. Then he suddenly thought of Polly's father.

He made his way to the back of the store and crossed the space separating the building from its neighbour, where the gunman had been concealed. The man's body lay where it had fallen. As Creed came round the corner he saw another body lying a little way off. He made his way to where it lay face down on the earth, bent down and turned it over. The corpse was that of a man of about fifty. Even in death Creed thought he could recognize a vague resemblance to the features of Polly. He remembered what he had heard on the rooftop and was pretty sure that he had found Polly's father.

The man had been wounded in a number of places and it was impossible to tell which side had fired the fatal shots. Creed stood up; coming towards him was Polly. She had her hand to her face and there was a wild look in her eyes. Moving slowly as if in a daze she came up to Creed, then looked down at the body.

'I'm sorry,' Creed said.

She looked up at him with tear-filled eyes; then, dropping to her knees, took the body in her arms and began to cradle it. Although she was silent Creed could see her shoulders shaking.

'He saved your life,' he said.

She turned her face up to him.

'That other man; he was going to shoot you,' he told her, 'but your father shot him first.'

The flicker of a smile lifted the corner of her mouth and she nodded almost imperceptibly before turning back to her burden. Creed waited for a few moments, uncertain what to do next. The whoops of the Indians, the firing of guns and the sound of galloping horses came to their ears but they were sheltered by the angle of the building and the sounds seemed to come from far away. Creed moved a little apart, turning away so as to leave Polly to her grief. Then he felt her come beside him. She took his arm and they walked together back to the shelter of the store.

It was late in the day. The sun was westering behind the high summit of Gaunt's Peak.

Peace had returned to the valley and down by the stream a big campfire had been lit. In the flickering light of its flames a group of people had gathered, consisting of the surviving prospectors, among whom were Creed and Polly together with Timber Wolf and White Fawn, and a small group of Sioux led by their chief, Akecheta.

The rest of the Indians had ridden away after taking their revenge on the outlaws and gunslicks who had brought them so much trouble. Creed had heard the story of Timber Wolf's defence of the pass. The big man and his group of prospectors had held the outlaws at bay for a long time before eventually being driven back by the sheer weight of opposing numbers. Timber Wolf's face carried the marks of buckshot and he was favouring a limp from the same shotgun blast.

Creed's shoulder was heavily bandaged. Polly had wanted to put his arm in a sling but he had drawn the line at the bandages.

White Fawn, for her part, seemed little the worse for her experience. Polly was holding herself well but Creed knew how she was hurting and that there were more tears to be shed. But time would ease the pain.

Behind them the Sioux had drawn up their horses

and Akecheta was making his farewells. Looking Creed in the eyes, he said something in the Lakota language to his interpreter. The brave turned to Creed.

'Akechetah say you are well named. Ohitekah mean brave and you are brave man.'

'Tell Akechetah I thank him on behalf of us all for his help and support. Without him we would not have emerged victorious.'

The Sioux brave interpreted and Akecheta's head bowed in acknowledgement. He spoke once more and again the interpreter translated.

'Akechetah say you have helped Sioux destroy bad men. You are always welcome in the tepees of his people.'

The Sioux chief extended his arm and, as they had done on the first occasion of their meeting, he exchanged salutations with Creed. Then he turned and, followed by his group of warriors, mounted his horse. They rode away without looking back. Creed turned to Polly and went to join Timber Wolf and White Fawn.

'What now?' the big man asked.

'Stay around for a few days, help you get this place put back to normal. Then, who knows?'

'I have found more than my father,' Polly said, smiling bravely. 'Now, it doesn't matter where we go.'

The voices of the prospectors calling them to join the group round the fire brought them back to present realities.

'By the way,' Timber Wolf said, 'if you're plannin' on goin' back to Tamarack Creek, don't forget to keep an eye out for the marshal.'

'It ain't the marshal I'd be worryin' about,' Creed replied. 'It's the oldster at the stage depot I'd be aimin' to avoid.' He paused. 'Although he still owes me somethin' for deliverin' the letters.'